THE STORY OF
A BAD BOY

BY THOMAS BAILEY ALDRICH
ILLUSTRATED BY
A. B. FROST

BOSTON AND NEW YORK

HOUGHTON MIFFLIN COMPANY

The Riverside Press Cambridge

" My name 's Bailey ', what' s your name ? "

Thomas Bailey Aldrich (November 11, 1836 – March 19, 1907) was an American writer, poet, critic, and editor. He is notable for his long editorship of The Atlantic Monthly, during which he published works by Charles W. Chesnutt and others. He was also known for his semi-autobiographical book The Story of a Bad Boy, which established the "bad boy's book" subgenre in nineteenth-century American literature,and for his poetry, which included "The Unguarded Gates"

A PREFACE, IN WHICH THE AUTHOR DECLINES TO WRITE ONE

THE Publishers of the pres-ent new edition of THE STORY OF A BAD BOY have requested my agency in the matter of procuring from the author a Few lines, by vway of intro- cl action. It soems to me

that the Bad Boy reqah.es no introduction to

a public that has tolerated frim for upwards of twenty years. Moreover, I am no believer in prefaces. The author who has not been able in the course of several hundred pages to say what he had to say is not likely to accomplish that feat in narrower compass. On consulting with the Bad Boy, I find this to be the view which he himself entertains. He claims that he faithfully performed the modest task he undertook, and is not con-

scious that anything in the narrative requires elucidation. As he concerned himself with little that did not come within the sphere of his own experience, he ran less risk of mak-ing mistakes than if he had attempted to write pure fiction. A generous destiny pro-vided him with ample materials for his auto-biography, and he invented next to nothing. The statement of this fact incidentally and economically answers the fifteen hundred or two thousand; insidious letter? which have been addressed to him" by autograph-hunters desiring to know: whether :u The Story of a

Bad Boy"

These are points, however, on which the author would probably not touch, could he be induced to write a preface. He would deal, rather, with the subsequent fate of the characters who lend what life there is to his little seaport comedy. With one exception they all have made their exit from that larger stage on which they moved more or less suc-cessfully. The exception is the Hon. Pepper

Whitcomb. The newspapers, which relieve our Chief Magistrates from the embarrass-ment of selecting cabinet officers, foreign ministers, collectors of the port, and other high public functionaries — the newspapers, I repeat, are at the present moment engaged in putting Pepper Whitcomb into the next vacancy that may occur on the bench of the Supreme Court of the United States. The historian of Rivermouth could have made much of this dignified circumstance, and much, also, of the singular fact that the old Temple Grammar School building was de-stroyed by fire, a number of years ago, in precisely the manner foretold in the story: a coincidence worth dwelling on. Perhaps, too, the author, with the chronic weakness peculiar to preface-writers — that sudden impulse which seizes them to give their own case away — might have been led to confess a doubt touching his wisdom in calling the book " The Story of a Bad Boy." He wished simply to draw a line at the start between

his hero — a natural, actual boy — and that unwholesome and altogether improbable lit-tle prig which had hitherto been held up as an example to the young. The title of the volume has doubtless turned aside manyexcellent persons who would have foundnothing seriously reprehensible in the volumeitself. On the other hand, this lurid titlemay have invited the curiosity of the viciousand depraved, and trapped them into readingan entirely harmless story. In which casethe author may felicitate himself on sowinga seed in the wider field, for the vicious out-number the virtuous ten to one. Besides,the virtuous need no missionary.

As the author has never evinced the faint-est regret in connection with the title chosen,he probably feels none, and it would be idleon my part to give further chase to a mereconjecture.

The poet Wordsworth, assisted by Plautus,maintains — to the everlasting confusion ofMr. Darwin — that " the good die first."

Perhaps this explains why the Bad Boy hassurvived so many good boys in the juvenileliterature of the last two decades. It onlypartly explains it, however. The secret ofhis persistence may be stated without cast-ing any shadow upon the general respec-tability of his character. Indeed, the secretwas long ago kindly disclosed by Mr. How-ells 1 when he said: " No one else seems tohave thought of telling the story of a boy'slife with so great desire to show what a boy'slife is, and with so little purpose of teachingwhat it should be; certainly no one else hasthought of doing this for the American boy."At the period when the author pennedthese chapters he was far enough away fromhis boyhood to regard it in retrospect, andyet not so far removed as to be beyond thelightest touch of its glamour. His attitudewas wholly without self-consciousness; nophotographer of manners had told him to" look natural;' he did not have one eye on

1 In The Atlantic Monthly for January, 1870.

his inkstand and the other on his public.He had a message, such as it was, and hedelivered it with as good grace as he could.If he wrote with little art, he wrote with suf-ficient sincerity, and it so chanced that heappealed directly not only to the sense ofyouthful readers, but to the sympathy of suchmen and women as still remembered thatthey once were young.

To these two classes the author again of-fers his unpretentious chronicle, now enrichedby sixty designs from the pencil of Mr. A. B.Frost, but otherwise unchanged. The writertells me that in supervising the sheets forthe press he has a hundred times beentempted to recast a page or a paragraph ;but there was a morning bloom upon thefaulty text, a bloom that he could not touchwithout destroying—a nameless quality ofunknowing youth, impossible to recapture,and for the lack of which no later art couldcompensate. T. B. A.

THE CRAGS,Tenant's Harbor, Maine,1894.

CONTENTS

THE STORY OF A BAD BOY

CHAPTER I

IN WHICH I INTRODUCE MYSELF

THIS is the story ofa bad boy. Well, notsuch a very bad, but apretty bad boy ; and Iought to know, for Iam, or rather I was,that boy myself.

Lest the title shouldmislead the reader, Ihasten to assure himhere that I have nodark confessions tomake. I call my storythe story of a bad boy,partly to distinguishmyself from thosefaultless young gentlemen who generally figure innarratives of this kind, and partly because I reallywas not a cherub. I may truthfully say I was anamiable, impulsive lad, blessed with fine digestivepowers, and no hypocrite. I did not want to bean angel and with the angels stand; I did not

Not a Cherub

think the missionary tracts presented to me bythe Rev. Wibird Hawkins were half so nice asRobinson Crusoe ; and I failed to send my littlepocket-money to the natives of the Feejee Islands,but spent it royally in peppermint-drops and taffycandy. In short, I was a real human boy, such as you may meet anywhere in New England, and no more like the impossible boy in a story-book than a sound orange is like one that has been sucked dry. But let us begin at the beginning.

Whenever a new scholar came to our school, I used to confront him at recess with the following words : " My name 's Tom Bailey; what's your name ? ' If the name struck me favorably, I shook hands with the new pupil cordially; but if it did not, I would turn on my heel, for I was particular on this point. Such names as Higgins, Wiggins, and Spriggins were deadly affronts to my ear; while Langdon, Wallace, Blake, and the like, were passwords to my confidence and esteem.

Ah me ! some of those dear fellows are rather elderly boys by this time — lawyers, merchants, sea-captains, soldiers, authors, what not ? Phil Adams (a special good name that Adams) is consul at Shanghai, where I picture him to myself with his head closely shaved — he never had too much hair — and a long pigtail hanging down behind. He is married, I hear ; and I hope he and she that was Miss Wang Wang are very happy together, sitting cross-legged over their diminutive cups of

IN WHICH I INTRODUCE MYSELF

Judge Pepper Whitcomb

tea in a sky-blue tower hung with bells. It is so I think of him ; to me he is henceforth a jeweled mandarin, talking nothing but broken China. Whit-comb is a judge, sedate and wise, with spectacles bal-anced on the bridge of that remarkable nose which, in former days, was so plenti-fully sprinkled with freckles that the boys christened him Pepper Whitcomb. Just to think of little Pepper Whit-comb being a judge ! What would he do to me now, I wonder, if I were to sing out " Pepper!" someday in court ? Fred Langdon is in California, in the native-wine business—he used to make the best licorice-water / ever tasted ! Binny Wallace sleeps in the Old South Burying-Ground; and Jack Harris, too, is dead — Harris, who com-manded us boys, of old, in the famous snow-ball battles of Slatter's Hill. Was it yesterday I saw him at the head of his regiment on its way to join the shattered Army of the Potomac ? Not yes-terday, but six years ago. It was at the battle of the Seven Pines. Gallant Jack Harris, that never drew rein until he had dashed into the Rebel battery ! So they found him — lying across the enemy's guns.

How we have parted, and wandered, and mar-ried, and died ! I wonder what has become of all the boys who went to the Temple Grammar School at Rivermouth when I was a youngster ?

" All, all are gone, the old familiar faces ! "

It is with no ungentle hand I summon them back, for a moment, from that Past which has closed upon them and upon me. How pleas-antly they live again in my memory! Happy, magical Past, in whose fairy atmosphere even Conway, mine ancient foe, stands forth transfig-ured, with a sort of dreamy glory encircling his bright red hair !

With the old school formula I begin these sketches of my boyhood. My name is Tom Bailey; what is yours, gentle reader ? I take for granted that it is neither Wiggins nor Spriggins, and thatwe shall get on famously together, and be capitalfriends forever.

CHAPTER II

IN WHICH I ENTERTAIN PECULIAR VIEWS

I WAS born at Rivermouth, but, before I had achance to become very well acquainted with thatpretty New England town, my parents removedto New Orleans, where my father invested hismoney so securely in the banking business thathe was never able to get more than half of it outagain. But of this hereafter.

I was only eighteen months old at the time ofthe removal, and it did not make much differenceto me where Iwas, because Iwas so small;but several yearslater, when myfather proposedto take me Northto be educated, Ihad my own pe-

J . Black Satn

culiar views on

the subject. I instantly kicked over the littlenegro boy who happened to be standing by meat the moment, and, stamping my foot violentlyon the floor of the piazza, declared that I would

 not be taken away to live among a lot of Yan-kees !

You see I was what is called " a Northern manwith Southern principles." I had no recollectionof New England: my earliest memories were con-nected with the South, with Aunt Chloe, my oldnegro nurse, and with the great ill-kept garden inthe centre of which stood our house — a white-washed brick house it was, with wide verandas —shut out from the street by lines of orange, fig,and magnolia trees. I knew I was born at theNorth, but hoped nobody would find it out. Ilooked upon the misfortune as something soshrouded by time and distance that maybe nobodyremembered it. I never told my schoolmates Iwas a Yankee, because they talked about theYankees in such a scornful way as to make mefeel that it was quite a disgrace not to be born inLouisiana, or at least in one of the Border States.And this impression was strengthened by AuntChloe, who said, " Dar ain't no gentl'men in theNorf noway," and on one occasion terrified mebeyond measure by declaring : " If any of demmean whites tries to git me away from marster,I's jes' gwine to knock 'em on de head wid agourd !"

The way this poor creature's eyes flashed, andthe tragic air with which she struck at an imagi-nary " mean white," are among the most vividthings in my memory of those days.

To be frank, my idea of the North was about asaccurate as that entertained by the well-educatedEnglishmen of the present day concerning Amer-ica. I supposed the inhabitants were divided intotwo classes — Indians and white people ; that theIndians occasionally dashed down on New York,and scalped any woman or child (giving the pref-erence to children) whom they caught lingering inthe outskirts after nightfall; that the white menwere either hunters or schoolmasters, and that itwas winter pretty much all the year round. Theprevailing style of architecture I took to be log-cabins.

With this delightful picture of Northern civili-zation in my eye, the reader will easily understandmy terror at the bare thought of being transportedto Rivermouth to school, and possibly will forgiveme for kicking over little black Sam, and other-wise misconducting myself, when my father an-nounced his determination to me. As for kickinglittle Sam — I always did that, more or less gen-tly, when anything went wrong with me.

My father was greatly perplexed and troubledby this unusually violent outbreak, and especiallyby the real consternation which he saw writtenin every line of my countenance. As little blackSam picked himself up, my father took my handin his and led me thoughtfully to the library.

I can see him now as he leaned back in thebamboo chair and questioned me. He appeared strangely agitated on learning the nature of myobjections to going North, and proceeded at onceto knock down all my pine-log houses, and scatter all the Indian tribes withwhich I had populated thegreater portion of the East-ern and Middle States.

"Who on earth, Tom/has filled your brain withsuch silly stories ?' askedmy father, wiping the tearsfrom his eyes.

"Aunt Chloe, sir; shetold me."

"And you really thoughtyour grandfather wore ablanket embroidered withbeads, and ornamented hisleggings with the scalps ofhis enemies ?""Well, sir, I did n't think that exactly.""Did n't think that exactly ? Tom, you will bethe death of me."

He hid his face in his handkerchief, and, whenhe looked up, he seemed to have been sufferingacutely. I was deeply moved myself, though I didnot clearly understand what I had said or done tocause him to feel so badly. Perhaps I had hurt hisfeelings by thinking it even possible that Grand-father Nutter was an Indian warrior.

My Indian Ancestor

My father devoted that evening and several sub-sequent evenings to giving me a clear and succinctaccount of New England ; its early struggles, itsprogress, and its present condition — faint and con-fused glimmerings of all which I had obtained atschool, where history had never been a favoritepursuit of mine.

" Tom, you will be the death of me "

I was no longer unwilling to go North ; on thecontrary, the proposed journey to a new world fullof wonders kept me awake nights. I promisedmyself all sorts of fun and adventures, though Iwas not entirely at rest in my mind touching the

10 THE STORY OF A BAD BOY

savages, and secretly resolved to go on board theship — the journey was to be made by sea — witha certain little brass pistol in my trousers pocket,in case of any difficulty with the tribes when welanded at Boston.

I could not get the Indian out of my head.Only a short time previously the Cherokees — orwas it the Camanches ? — had been removed fromtheir hunting-grounds in Arkansas ; and in thewilds of the Southwest the red men were still asource of terror to the border settlers. " Troublewith the Indians' was the staple news fromFlorida published in the New Orleans papers. Wewere constantly hearing of travelers being attackedand murdered in the interior of that State. Ifthese things were done in Florida, why not inMassachusetts ?

Yet long before the sailing day arrived I waseager to be off. My impatience was increased bythe fact that my father had purchased for me a finelittle mustang pony, and shipped it to Rivermoutha fortnight previous to the date set for our owndeparture—for both my parents were to accom-pany me. The pony (which nearly kicked me outof bed one night in a dream), and my father'spromise that he and my mother would come toRivermouth every other summer, completely re-signed me to the situation. The pony's namewas Gitana, which is the Spanish for gypsy; so Ialways called her — she was a lady pony — Gypsy.

IN WHICH I ENTERTAIN PECULIAR VIEWS II

At last the time came to leave the vine-cov-ered mansion among the orange-trees, to say good-by to little black Sam (I am convinced he washeartily glad to get rid of me), and to part withsimple Aunt Chloe, who, in the confusion of hergrief, kissed an eyelash into my eye, and thenburied her face in the bright bandana turbanwhich she had mounted that morning in honor ofour departure.

I fancy them standing by the open garden gate ;the tears are rolling down Aunt Chloe's cheeks ;Sam's six front teeth are glistening like pearls; Iwave my hand to him manfully, then I call out"good-by" in a muffled voice to Aunt Chloe;they and the old home fade away. I am never tosee them again!

CHAPTER III

ON BOARD THE TYPHOON

I DO not remember much about the voyage toBoston, for after the first few hours at sea I wasdreadfully unwell.

The name of our ship was the "A No. i, fast-sailing packet Typhoon." I learned afterwardsthat she sailed fast only in the newspaper adver-tisements. My father owned one quarter of theTyphoon, and that is why we happened to go inher. I tried to guess which quarter of the ship heowned, and finally concluded it must be the hindquarter—the cabin, in which we had the cosiestof staterooms, with one round window in the roof,and two shelves or boxes nailed up against thewall to sleep in.

There was a good deal of confusion on deckwhile we were getting under way. The captainshouted orders (to which nobody seemed to payany attention) through a battered tin trumpet, andgrew so red in the face that he reminded me of ascooped-out pumpkin with a lighted candle inside.He swore right and left at the sailors without theslightest regard for their feelings. They didn'tmind it a bit, however, but went on singing:

" Heave ho!

With the rum below,And hurrah for the Spanish Main OI "

I will not be positive about " the Spanish Main,"but it was hurrah for something O. I consideredthem very jolly fel-lows, and so, indeed,they were. Oneweather-beaten tar inparticular struck myfancy — a thick-set,jovial man, about fiftyyears of age, withtwinkling blue eyesand a fringe of grayhair circling his headlike a crown. As hetook off his tarpaulinI observed that thetop of his head wasquite smooth and flat, as if somebody had sat downon him when he was very young.

There was something noticeably hearty in thisman's bronzed face, a heartiness that seemed toextend to his loosely knotted neckerchief. Butwhat completely won my good will was a pictureof enviable loveliness painted on his left arm. Itwas the head of a woman with the body of a fish.Her flowing hair was of livid green, and she helda pink comb in one hand. I never saw anything

The Captain

so beautiful. I determined to know that man. Ithink I would have given my brass pistol to havehad such a picture painted on my arm.

While I stood admiring this work of art, a fat,wheezy steam-tug, with the word AJAX in staringblack letters on the paddle-box, came purring upalongside the Typhoon. It was ridiculously small ^and conceited, compared with our stately ship. Ispeculated as to what it was going to do. In afew minutes we were lashed to the little monster,which gave a snort and a shriek, and began back-ing us out from the levee (wharf) with the greatestease.

I once saw an ant running away with a piece ofcheese eight or ten times larger than itself. Icould not help thinking of it, when I found thechubby, smoky-nosed tug-boat towing the Typhoonout into the Mississippi River.

In the middle of the stream we swung round,the current caught us, and away we flew like agreat winged bird. Only it did not seem as if wewere moving. The shore, with the countlesssteamboats, the tangled rigging of the ships, andthe long lines of warehouses, appeared to be glid-ing away from us.

It was grand sport to stand on the quarter-deckand watch all this. Before long there was nothingto be seen on either side but stretches of lowswampy land, covered with stunted cypress-trees,from which drooped delicate streamers of Spanish

moss —a fine place for alligators and congo snakes.Here and there we passed a yellow sand-bar, andhere and there a snag lifted its nose out of thewater like a shark.

" This is your last chance to see the city, Tom,"said my father, as we swept round a bend of theriver.

I turned and looked. New Orleans was just acolorless mass of something in the distance, andthe dome of the St. Charles Hotel, upon which thesun shimmered for a moment, was no bigger thanthe top of old Aunt Chloe's thimble.

What do I remember next ? the gray sky andthe fretful blue waters of the Gulf. The steam-tughad long since let slip her hawsers and gone pant-ing away with a derisive scream, as much as tosay, " I 've done my duty, now look out for your,self, old Typhoon ! "

The ship seemed quite proud of being left totake care of itself, and, with its huge white sailsbulged out, strutted off like a vain turkey. I hadbeen standing by my father near the wheel-houseall this while, observing things with that nicetyof perception which belongs only to children ; butnow the dew began falling, and we went below tohave supper.

The fresh fruit and milk, and the slices of coldchicken looked very nice; yet somehow I had noappetite. There was a general smell of tar abouteverything. Then the ship gave sudden lurches

i6

THE STORY OF A BAD BOY

that made it a matter of uncertainty whether onewas going to put his fork to his mouth or intohis eye. The tumblers and wineglasses, stuck ina rack over the table, kept clinking and clinking ;and the cabin lamp, suspended by four gilt chainsfrom the ceiling, swayed to and fro crazily. Nowthe floor seemed to rise, and now it seemed to sinkunder one's feet like a feather-bed.

There were not more than a dozen passengerson board, including ourselves; and all of these,excepting a bald-headed old gentleman — a retiredsea-captain — disappeared into their staterooms atan early hour of the evening.

After supper was cleared away, my father and

the elderly gentleman,whose name was Cap-tain Truck, played atcheckers ; and I amusedmyself for a while bywatching the troublethey had in keeping themen in the properplaces. Just at the mostexciting point of thegame, the ship wouldcareen, and down would go the white checkerspell-mell among the black. Then my fatherlaughed, but Captain Truck would grow very an-gry, and vow that he would have won the game ina move or two more, if the confounded old

chicken*

Playing Checkers

coop — that's what he called the ship — hadn'tlurched.

"I — I think I will go to bed now, please," Isaid, laying my hand on my father's knee, and feel-ing exceedingly queer.

It was high time, for the Typhoon was plungingabout in the most alarming fashion. I was speed-ily tucked away in the upper berth, where I felt atrifle more easy at first. My clothes were placedon a narrow shelf at my feet, and it was a greatcomfort to me to know that my pistol was sohandy, for I made no doubt we should fall in withpirates before many hours. This is the last thingI remember with any distinctness. At midnight,as I was afterwards told, we were struck by a galewhich never left us until we came in sight of theMassachusetts coast.

For days and days I had no sensible idea ofwhat was going on around me. That we werebeing hurled somewhere upside-down, and that Idid not like it, was about all I knew. I have, in-deed, a vague impression that my father used toclimb up to the berth and call me his " AncientMariner," bidding me cheer up. But the AncientMariner was far from cheering up, if I recollect!rightly; and I do not believe that venerable navi-igator would have cared much if it had been an-'nounced to him, through a speaking-trumpet, that" a low, black, suspicious craft, with raking masts,was rapidly bearing down upon us!"

In fact, one morning, I thought that such wasthe case, for bang! went the big cannon I hadnoticed in the bow of the ship when we came onboard, and which had suggested to me the idea ofpirates. Bang! went the gun again in a few sec-onds. I made a feeble effort to get at my trouserspocket. But the Typhoon was only saluting CapeCod — the first land sighted by vessels approach-ing the coast from a southerly direction.

The vessel had ceased to roll, and my seasick-ness passed away as rapidly as it came. I was allright now, " only a little shaky in my timbers anda little blue about the gills," as Captain Truckremarked to my mother, who, like myself, hadbeen confined to the stateroom during the passage.

At Cape Cod the wind parted company with uswithout saying as much as " Excuse me;" so wewere nearly two days in making the run which infavorable weather is usually accomplished in sevenhours. That's what the pilot said.

I was able to go about the ship now, and I lostno time in cultivating the acquaintance of thesailor with the green-haired lady on his arm. Ifound him in the forecastle — a sort of cellar inthe front part of the vessel. He was an agreeablesailor, as I had expected, and we became the bestof friends in five minutes.

He had been all over the world two or threetimes, and knew no end of stories. According tohis own account, he must have been shipwreckei

at least twice a year ever since his birth. He hadserved under Decatur when that gallant officerpeppered the Algerines and made them promise not

In the Forecastle

to sell their prisoners of war into slavery ; he hadworked a gun at the bombardment of Vera Cruzin the Mexican War, and he had been on Alexan-der Selkirk's Island more than once. There were

20 THE STORY OF A BAD BOY

very few things he had not done in a seafaringway.

" I suppose, sir," I remarked, " that ycur nameisn't Typhoon ?"

" Why, Lord love ye, lad, my name's JBenjaminWatson, of Nantucket. But I 'm a true bl' ^ Ty-phooner," he added, which increased my ^ctfor him; I do not know why, and I did ncthen whether Typhoon was the name of a ,ble or a profession.

Not wishing to be outdone in frankue"*closed to him that my name was Tom Ba'which he said he was very glad to hear ;

When we got more intimate, I discov

Saijor Ben, as he wished me to cs (>ii^perfect walking picture-book. He hf;chors, a star, and a frigate in full sail o'u nisarm; a pair of lovely blue hands clasr"-;' obreast, and I have no doubt that other parts rj v'sbody were illustrated in the same agreeablner. I imagine 'e was fond of drawings, ai okthis means of gratifying his artistic taste. wascertainly very ingenious and convenient. A port-folio might be displaced, or dropped overboard ;but Sailor Ben had his pictures wherever he went,just as that eminent pei^on in the m

" With rings on her fingers ano bells on -es "

was accompanied by music on all occ

The two hands on his breast, he .ormcd me,were a tribute to the memory of a dead mess--

ON BOARD THE TYPHOON 21

mate from whom he had parted years ago — andsurely t. more teaching tribute was never engrave.don a tombstone. This caused me to think of myparting with old Aunt Chloe, and I told him Ishould take it as a great favor indeed if he wouldpain' ~ "->ink hand and a black hand on my chest..H" lthe colors were pricked into the skin withand that the operation was somewhatpamHii. I assured him, in an off-hand manner,<•' T did . f mind pain, and begged him to set to" ' '"nee.pie-hearted fellow, who was proba'blyVain of his skill, took me into the fore-.'* TTr)s on the point of complying with my*hc- my father happened to look down

the ail a circumstance that rather inter-

fe vith the decorative art.

I have another opportunity of conferring

ar ' rith Sailor Ben, for the next morning, brightai* Jy, we came in sight of the cupola of the

Bos'i State House.

CHAPTER IV

RIVERMOUTH

IT was a beautiful May morning when the Ty-phoon hauled up at Long Wharf. Whether theIndians were not early risers, or whether theywere away just then on a war-path, I could notdetermine ; but they did not appear in any greatforce — in fact, did not appear at all.

In the remarkable geography which I neverhurt myself with studying at New Orleans was apicture representing the landing of the PilgrimFathers at Plymouth. The Pilgrim Fathers, inrather odd hats and coats, are seen approachingthe savages ; the savages, in no coats or hatsto speak of, are evidently undecided whether toshake hands with the Pilgrim Fathers or to makeone grand rush and scalp the entire party. Nowthis scene had so stamped itself on my mind that,in spite of all my father had said, I was preparedfor some such greeting from the aborigines.Nevertheless, I was not sorry to have my expec-tations unfulfilled. By the way, speaking of thePilgrim Fathers, I often used to wonder why therewas no mention made of the Pilgrim Mothers.

While our trunks were being hoisted from the

hold of the ship, I mounted on the roof of thecabin, and took a critical view of Boston. As wecame up the harbor, I had noticed that the houseswere huddled together on an immense hill, at thetop of which was a large building, the StateHouse, towering proudly above the rest, like anamiable mother-hen surrounded by her brood ofmany-colored chickens. A closer inspection didnot impress me very favorably. The city wasnot nearly so imposing as New Orleans, whichstretches out for miles and miles, in the shape ofa crescent, along the banks of the majestic river.

I soon grew tired of looking at the masses ofhouses, rising above one another in irregular tiers,and was glad my father did not propose to remainlong in Boston. As I leaned over the rail in thismood, a measly-looking little boy with no shoessaid that if I would come down on the wharf hewould lick me for two cents — not an exorbitantprice. But I did not go down. I climbed intothe rigging, and stared at him. This, as I wasrejoiced to observe, so exasperated him that hestood on his head on a pile of boards, in order topacify himself.

The first train for Rivermouth left at noon.After a late breakfast on board the Typhoon, oultrunks were piled upon a baggage-wagon, and our-selves stowed away in a coach, which must haveturned at least one hundred corners before it setus down at the railway station.

In less time than it takes to tell it, we wereshooting across the country at a fearful rate — nowclattering over a bridge, now screaming through atunnel; here we cut a flourishing village in two,like a knife, and here we dived into the shadow ofa pine forest. Sometimes we glided along theedge of the ocean, and could see the sails of shipstwinkling like bits of silver against the horizon ;sometimes we dashed across rocky pasture-landswhere stupid-eyed cattle were loafing. It was funto scare the lazy-looking cows that lay round ingroups under the newly budded trees near therailroad track.

We did not pause at any of the little brown sta-tions on the route (they looked just like overgrownblack-walnut clocks), though at every one of thema man popped out as if he were worked by ma-"chinery, and waved a red flag, and appeared asthough he would like to have us stop. But wewere an express train, and made no stoppages, ex-cepting once or twice to give the engine a drink.

It is strange how the memory clings to somethings. It is over twenty years since I took thatfirst ride to Rivermouth, and yet, oddly enough,I remember as if it were yesterday that, as wepassed slowly through the village of Hampton, wesaw two boys fighting behind a red barn. Therewas also a shaggy yellow dog, who looked as ifhe had begun to unravel, barking himself all upinto a knot with excitement. We had only a hur-

ried glimpse of the battle — long enough, however,to see that the combatants were equally matchedand very much in earnest. I am ashamed to sayhow many times since I have speculated as towich boy got licked. Maybe both the smallrascals are dead now (not in consequence of theset-to, let us hope), or maybe they are married,and have pug-nacious urchins iof their own;yet to this dayI sometimesfind myself won-dering how thatfight turnedout.

We had beenriding perhapstwo hours anda half, when weshot by a tallfactory with achimney resembling a church-steeple ; then the lo-comotive gave a scream, the engineer rang his bell,and we plunged into the twilight of a long woodenbuilding, open at both ends. Here we stopped,and the conductor, thrusting his head in at the cardoor, cried out, " Passengers for Rivermouth !"

At last we had reached our journey's end. Onthe platform my father shook hands with a

A Glimpse of the Battle

Straight, brisk old gentleman, whose face was veryserene and rosy. He had on a white hat and along swallow-tailed coat, the collar of which cameclear up above his ears. He did not look unlikea Pilgrim Father. This, of course, was Grand-father Nutter, at whose house I was born. Mymother kissed him a great many times; and I wasglad to see him myself, though I naturally did notfeel very intimate with a person whom I had notseen since I was eighteen months old.

While we were getting into the double-seatedwagon which Grandfather Nutter had provided,I took the opportunity of asking after the healthof the pony. The pony had arrived all right tendays before, and was in the stable at home, quiteanxious to see me.

As we drove through the quiet old town, Ithought Rivermouth the prettiest place in theworld; and I think so still. The streets are longand wide, shaded by gigantic American elms,whose drooping branches, interlacing here andthere, span the avenue with arches gracefulenough to be the handiwork of fairies. Many ofthe houses have small flower-gardens in front, gayin the season with china-asters, and are substan-tially built, with massive chimney-stacks and pro-truding eaves. A beautiful river goes rippling bythe town, and, after turning and twisting amonga lot of tiny islands, empties itself into the sea.

The harbor is so fine that the largest ships can

sail directly up to the wharves and drop anchor.Only they do not. Years ago it was a famous sea-port. Princely fortunes were made in the WestIndia trade; and in 1812, when we were at warwith Great Britain, any number of privateers werefitted out at Rivermouth to prey upon the mer-chant vessels of the enemy. Certain people grewsuddenly and mysteriously rich. A great manyof " the first families ' of to-day do not care totrace their pedigree back to the time when theirgrandsires owned shares in the Matilda Jane,twenty-four guns.

Few ships come to Rivermouth now. Com-merce drifted into other ports. The phantomfleet sailed off one day, and never came backagain. The crazy old warehouses are empty ; andbarnacles and eelgrass cling to the piles of thecrumbling wharves, where the sunshine lies lov-ingly, bringing out the faint spicy odor thathaunts the place — the ghost of the old dead WestIndia trade.

During our ride from the station, I was struck,of course, only by the general neatness of thehouses and the beauty of the elm-trees lining thestreets. I describe Rivermouth now as I came toknow it afterwards.

Rivermouth is a very ancient town. In my daythere existed a tradition among the boys that itwas here Christopher Columbus made his firstlanding on this continent. I remember having

the exact spot pointed out to me by PepperWhitcomb. One thing is certain, Captain JohnSmith, who afterwards, according to their legend,married Pocahontas — whereby he got Powhatanfor a father-in-law — explored the river in 1614,and was much charmed by the beauty of River-mouth, which at that time was covered with wildstrawberry-vines.

Rivermouth figures prominently in all the colo-nial histories. Every other house in the place hasits tradition more or less grim and entertaining.If ghosts could flourish anywhere, there are cer-tain streets in Rivermouth that would be full ofthem. I do not know of a town with so many oldhouses. Let us linger, for a moment, in front ofthe one which the Oldest Inhabitant is alwayssure to point out to the curious stranger.

It is a square wooden edifice, with gambrelroof and deep-set window-frames. Over the win-dows and doors there used to be heavy carvings —oak-leaves and acorns, and angels' heads withwings spreading from the ears, oddly jumbledtogether; but these ornaments and other outwardsigns of grandeur have long since disappeared.A peculiar interest attaches itself to this house,not because of its age, for it has not been stand-ing quite a century; nor on account of its archi-tecture, which is not striking — but because of theillustrious men who at various periods have occu-pied its spacious chambers.

29

In 1770 it was an aristocratic hotel. At theleft side of the entrance stood a high post, fromwhich swung the sign of the Earl of Halifax. Thelandlord was a stanchloyalist — that is tosay, he believed in theking, and when theovertaxed colonies de-termined to throw offthe British yoke, theadherents to the Crownheld private meetingsin one of the backrooms of the tavern.This irritated the reb-els, as they werecalled; and one night Tkt Vanishing Landlord

they made an attack on

the Earl of Halifax, tore down the signboard, brokein the window-sashes, and gave the landlord hardlytime to make himself invisible over a fence in therear.

For several months the shattered tavern ^re-mained deserted. At last the exiled innkeeper, onpromising to do better, was allowed to return ; anew sign, bearing the name of William Pitt, thefriend of America, swung proudly from the door-post, and the patriots were appeased. Here itwas that the mail-coach from Boston twice a week,for many a year, set down its load of travelers and

 gossip. For some of the details in this sketch, Iam indebted to a recently published chronicle ofthose times.

It is 1782. The French fleet is lying in theharbor of Rivermouth, and eight of the principalofficers, in white uniforms trimmed with gold lace,have taken up their quarters at the sign of theWilliam Pitt. Who is this young and handsomeofficer now entering the door of the tavern ? It isno less a personage than the Marquis Lafayette,who has come all the way from Providence to visitthe French gentlemen boarding there. What agallant-looking cavalier he is, with his quick eyesand coal-black hair ! Forty years later he visitedthe spot again ; his locks were gray and his stepwas feeble, but his heart held its young love forLiberty.

Who is this finely dressed traveler alightingfrom his coach-and-four, attended by servants inlivery ? Do you know that sounding name, writtenin big valorous letters on the Declaration of Inde-pendence — written as if by the hand of a giant ?Can you not see it now ? — JOHN HANCOCK. Thisis he.

Three young men, with their valet, are standing on the door-step of the William Pitt, bowingpolitely, and inquiring in the most courteous termsin the world if they can be accommodated. Itis the time of the French Revolution, and theseare three sons of the Duke of Orleans — Louis

Philippe and his two brothers. Louis Philippenever forgot his visit to Rivermouth. Yearsafterwards, when he was seated on the throne ofFrance, he asked an American lady, who chancedto be at his court, if the pleasant old mansion wasstill standing.

But a greater and a better man than the king ofthe French has honored this roof. Here, in 1789,came George Washington, the President of theUnited States, to pay his final complimentary visitto the State dignitaries. The wainscoted cham-ber where he slept, and the dining-hall where heentertained his guests, have a certain dignity andsanctity which even the present Irish tenantscannot wholly destroy.

During the period of my reign at Rivermouth,an ancient lady, Dame Jocelyn by name, lived inone of the upper rooms of this notable building.She was a dashing young belle at the time ofWashington's first visit to the town, and musthave been exceedingly coquettish and pretty, judg-ing from a certain portrait on ivory still in thepossession of the family. According to DameJocelyn, George Washington flirted with her justa little bit — in what a stately and highly finishedmanner can be imagined.

There was a mirror with a deep filigreed framehanging over the mantel-piece in this room. Theglass was cracked and the quicksilver rubbed offor discolored in many places. When it reflected

32 THE STORY OF A BAD BOY

your face, you had the singular pleasure of notrecognizing yourself. It gave your features theappearance of having been run through a mince-meat machine. But what rendered the looking-glass a thing of enchantment to me was a fadedgreen feather, tipped with scarlet, which droopedfrom the top of the tarnished gilt mouldings.This feather Washington took from the plume ofhis three-cornered hat, and presented with hisown hand to the worshipful Mistress Jocelyn theday he left Rivermouth forever. I wish I coulddescribe the mincing genteel air, and the ill-con-cealed self-complacency, with which the dear oldlady related the incident.

Many a Saturday afternoon have I climbed upthe rickety staircase to that dingy room, whichalways had a flavor of snuff about it, to sit on astiff-backed chair and listen for hours together toDame Jocelyn's stories of the olden time. Howshe would prattle! She was bedridden — poorcreature ! — and had not been out of the chamberfor fourteen years. Meanwhile the world had shotahead of Dame Jocelyn. The changes that hadtaken place under her very nose were unknown tothis faded, crooning old gentlewoman, whom theeighteenth century had neglected to take away with' * rest of its odd traps. She had no patiencenew-fangled notions. The old ways and the^L, nes were good enough for her. She hadnevei seen a steam-engine, though she had heard

RIVERMOUTH

33

" the dratted thing " screech in the distance. In her day, when gentlefolk traveled, they went in their own coaches. She did not see how respectable people could bring themselves down to " riding in a car with rag-tag and bobtail and Lord-knows-who." Poor old aristocrat! the landlord charged her no rent for the room, and the neighbors took turns in supplying her with meals. Towards the close of her life—she lived to be ninety-nine — she grew very fretful and capricious about her food. If she did not chance to fancy what was sent her, she had no hesitation in sending it back to the giver with " Miss Jocelyn's respectful compliments."

But I have beengossiping too long —and yet not too longif I have impressedupon the reader an idea of what a rusty, delightfulold town it was to which I had come to spend thenext three or four years of my boyhood.

A drive of twenty minutes from the stat" *brought us to the door-step of Grandfatherter's house. What kind of house it was, ary;ijsort of people lived in it, shall be told inchapter.

Miss Jocelyn's respectful compliments "

CHAPTER V
THE NUTTER HOUSE AND THE NUTTER FAMILY

THE Nutter House — all the more prominentdwellings in Rivermouth are named after some-body ; for instance, there is the Walford House,Jhe Venner House, the Trefethen House, etc.,though it by no means follows that they areinhabited by the people whose names they bear — the Nutter House, to resume, has been in ourfamily nearly a hundred years, and is an honor tothe builder (an ancestor of ours, I believe), sup-posing durability to be a merit. If our ancestorwas a carpenter, he knew his trade. I wish Iknew mine as well. Such timber and such work-manship do not often come together in housesbuilt nowadays.

Imagine a low-studded structure, with a widehall running through the middle. At your righthand, as you enter, stands a tall black mahoganyclock, looking like an Egyptian mummy set up onend. On each side of the hall are doors (whoseknobs, it must be confessed, do not turn veryeasily), opening into large rooms wainscoted andrich in wood-carvings about the mantel-pieces andcornices. The walls are covered with pictured

paper, representing landscapes and sea-views. Inthe parlor, for example, this enlivening figure isrepeated all over the room : A group of Englishpeasants, wearing Italian hats, are dancing on alawn that abruptly resolves itself into a sea-beach,upon which stands a flabby fisherman (nationalityunknown), quietly hauling in what appears to bea small whale, and totally regardless of the dread-ful naval combat going on just beyond the end ofhis fishing-rod. On the other side of the ships isthe mainland again, with the same peasants dan-cing. Our ancestors were very worthy people, buttheir wall-papers were abominable.

There are neither grates nor stoves in thesequaint chambers, but splendid open chimney-places, with room enough for the corpulent back-log to turn over comfortably on the polished and-irons. A wide staircase leads from the hall to thesecond story, which is arranged much like the first.Over this is the garret. I need not tell a New Eng-land boy what a museum of curiosities is the gar-ret of a well-regulated New England house of fiftyor sixty years' standing. Here meet together, asif by some preconcerted arrangement, all the bro-ken-down chairs of the household, all the spavinedtables, all the seedy hats, all the intoxicated-lookingboots, all the split walking-sticks that have retiredfrom business, " weary with the march of life."The pots, the pans, the trunks, the bottles — whomay hope to make an inventory of the number-

less odds and ends collected in this bewilderinglumber-room ? But what a place it is to sit of anafternoon with the rain pattering on the roof ! whata place in which to read Gulliver's Travels, or thefamous adventures of Rinaldo Rinaldini !

My grandfather's house stood a little back fromthe main street, in the shadow of two handsomeelms, whose overgrown boughs would dash them-selves against the gables whenever the wind blewhard. In the rear was a pleasant garden, coveringperhaps a quarter of an acre, full of plum-trees andgooseberry-bushes. These trees were old settlers,and are all dead now, excepting one, which bearsa purple plum as big as an egg. This tree, as Iremark, is still standing, and a more beautiful treeto tumble out of never grew anywhere. In thenorthwestern corner of the garden were the stablesand carriage-house, opening upon a narrow lane.You may imagine that I made an early visit to thatlocality to inspect Gypsy. Indeed, I paid her avisit every half-hour during the first day of my ar-rival. At the twenty-fourth visit she trod on myfoot rather heavily, as a reminder, probably, that Iwas wearing out my welcome. She was a knowinglittle pony, that Gypsy, and I shall have much tosay of her in the course of these pages.

Gypsy's quarters were all that could be wished,but nothing among my new surroundings gave memore satisfaction than the cosy sleeping apartmentthat had been prepared for myself. It was the hallroom over the front door.

THE NUTTER HOUSE AND THE FAMILY 37

I had never before had a chamber all to myself,and this one, about twice the size of our state-roomon board the Typhoon, was a marvel of neatnessand comfort. Pretty chintz curtains hung at thewindow, and a patch quilt of more colors than werein Joseph's coat covered thelittle truckle-bed. The pat-tern of the wall-paper left no-thing to be desired in that line.On a gray background weresmall bunches of leaves, un-like any that ever grew in thisworld; and on every other

"A fine black eye"

bunch perched a yellow-bird,pitted with crimson spots, as if it had just recov-ered from a severe attack of the small-pox. Thatno such bird ever existed did not detract from myadmiration of each one. There were two hundredand sixty-eight of these birds in all, not countingthose split in two where the paper was badly joined.I counted them once when I was laid up witha fine black eye, and falling asleep immediatelydreamed that the whole flock suddenly took wingand flew out of the window. From that time I wasnever able to regard them as merely inanimateobjects.

A wash-stand in the corner, a chest of carvedmahogany drawers, a looking-glass in a filigreedframe, and a high-backed chair studded withbrass nails like a coffin, constituted the furniture,

38 THE STORY OF A BAD BOY

Over the head of the bed were two oak shelves,holding perhaps a dozen books — among whichwere Theodore, or The Peruvians ; Robinson Cru-soe ; an odd volume of Tristram Shandy ; Baxter'sSaints' Rest, and a fine English edition of the Ara-bian Nights, with six hundred wood-cuts by Harvey.

Shall I ever forget the hour when I first over-hauled these books ? I do not allude especiallyto Baxter's Saints' Rest, which is far from beinga lively work for the young, but to the ArabianNights, and particularly Robinson Crusoe. Thethrill that ran into my fingers' ends then has not runout yet. Many a time did I steal up to this nestof a room, and, taking the dog's-eared volume fromits shelf, glide off into an enchanted realm, wherethere were no lessons to get and no boys to smashmy kite. In a lidless trunk in the garret I subse-quently unearthed another motley collection of nov-els and romances, embracing the adventures ofBaron Trenck, Jack Sheppard, Don Quixote, GilBias, and Charlotte Temple — all of which I fedupon like a bookworm.

I never come across a copy of any of those workswithout feeling a certain tenderness for the yellow-haired little rascal who used to lean above themagic pages hour after hour, religiously believingevery word he read, and no more doubting thereality of Sindbad the Sailor, or the Knight of theSorrowful Countenance, than he did the existenceof his own grandfather.

A Rainy Afternoon in the Garret

Against the wall at the foot of the bed hung asingle-barrel shot-gun — placed there by Grand-father Nutter, who knew what a boy loved, if evera grandfather did. As the trigger of the gun hadbeen accidentally twisted off, it was not, perhaps,the most dangerous weapon that could be placedin the hands of youth. In this maimed conditionits bump of destructiveness was much less thanthat of my small brass pocket-pistol, which I atonce proceeded to suspend from one of the nailssupporting the fowling-piece, for my vagaries con-cerning the red man had been entirely dispelled.

Having introduced the reader to the NutterHouse, a presentation to the Nutter family nat-urally follows. The family consisted of my grand-father; his sister, Miss Abigail Nutter; and KittyCollins, the maid-of-all-work.

Grandfather Nutter was a hale, cheery old gentle-man, as straight and as bald as an arrow. He hadbeen a sailor in early life; that is to say, at the ageof ten years he fled from the multiplication-table,and ran away to sea. A single voyage satisfiedhim. There never was but one of our family whodid not run away to sea, and this one died at hisbirth. My grandfather had also been a soldier —a captain of militia in 1812. If I owe the Britishnation anything, I owe thanks to that particularBritish soldier who put a musket-ball into the fleshypart of Captain Nutter's leg, causing that noblewarrior a slight permanent limp, but offsetting the

injury by furnishing him with material for a storywhich the old gentleman was never weary of tellingand I never weary of listening to. The story, inbrief, was as follows.

At the breaking out of the war, an English fri-gate lay for several days off the coast near River-mouth. A strong fort defended the harbor, and aregiment of minute-men, scattered at various pointsalongshore, stood ready to repel the boats, shouldthe enemy try to effect a landing. Captain Nut-ter had charge of a slight earthwork just outsidethe mouth of the river. Late one thick night thesound of oars was heard ; the sentinel tried to fireoff his gun at half-cock, and could not, when CaptainNutter sprung upon the parapet in the pitch dark-ness, and shouted, " Boat ahoy !' A musket-shotimmediately embedded itself in the calf of his leg.The Captain tumbled into the fort, and the boat,which had probably come in search of water, pulledback to the frigate.

This was my grandfather's only exploit duringthe war. That his prompt and bold conduct wasinstrumental in teaching the enemy the hopeless-ness of attempting to conquer such a people wasamong the firm beliefs of my boyhood.

At the time I came to Rivermouth my grand-father had retired from active pursuits, and wasliving at ease on his money, invested principallyin shipping. He had been a widower many years;a maiden sister, the aforesaid Miss Abigail, man-aging his household. Miss Abigail also managedher brother, and her brother's servant, and the vis-itor at her brother's gate — not in a tyrannical

Miss A bigail and Kitty Collins

spirit, but from a philanthropic desire to be usefulto everybody. In person she was tall and angu-lar ; she had a gray complexion, gray eyes, grayeyebrows, and generally wore a gray dress. Herstrongest weak point was a belief in the efficacyof " hot-drops " as a cure for all known diseases.If there were ever two persons who seemed to

dislike each other, Miss Abigail and Kitty Collinswere those persons. If ever two persons reallyloved each other, Miss Abigail and Kitty Collinswere those persons also. They were always eitherskirmishing or having a cup of tea lovingly to-gether.

Miss Abigail was very fond of me, and so wa*Kitty ; and in the course of their disagreementseach let me into the private history of the other.

According to Kitty, it was not originally mygrandfather's intention to have Miss Abigail atthe head of his domestic establishment. She hadswooped down on him (Kitty's own words), with aband-box in one hand and a faded blue cottonumbrella, still in existence, in the other. Clad inthis singular garb — I do not remember that Kittyalluded to any additional peculiarity of dress —Miss Abigail had made her appearance at thedoor of the Nutter House on the morning of mygrandmother's funeral. The small amount of bag-gage which the lady brought with her would haveled the superficial observer to infer that Miss Abi-gail's visit was limited to a few days. I run aheadof my story in saying she remained seventeenyears! How much longer she would have re-mained can never be definitely known now, as shedied at the expiration of that period.

Whether or not my grandfather was quitepleased by this unlooked-for addition to his familyis a problem. He was very kind always to Miss

Abigail, and seldom opposed her; though I thinkshe must have tried his patience sometimes, es-pecially when she interfered with Kitty.

Kitty Collins, or Mrs. Catherine, as she per-ferred to be called, was descended in a direct linefrom an extensive family of kings who formerlyruled over Ireland. In consequence of variouscalamities, among which the failure of the potato-crop may be mentioned, Miss Kitty Collins, incompany with several hundred of her countrymenand countrywomen — also descended from kings— came over to America in an emigrant ship, inthe year eighteen hundred and something

I do not know what freak of fortune caused theroyal exile to turn up at Rivermouth ; but turnup she did, a few months after arriving in thiscountry, and was hired by my grandmother to do"general housework" for the modest sum of fourshillings and sixpence a week.

Kitty had been living about seven years in mygrandfather's family when she unburdened herheart of a secret which had been weighing uponit all that time. It may be said of people, as it issaid of nations, " Happy are they that have no his-tory." Kitty had a history, and a pathetic one, Ithink.

On board the emigrant ship that brought herto America, she became acquainted with a sailor,who, being touched by Kitty's forlorn condition,was very good to her. Long before the end of the

46 THE STORY OF A BAD BOY

voyage, which had been tedious and perilous, shewas heart-broken at the thought of separatingfrom her kindly protector; but they were not topart just yet, for the sailor returned Kitty's affec-tion, and the two were married on their arrival atport. Kitty's husband — she would never men-tion his name, but kept it locked in her bosomlike some precious relic — had a considerable sumof money when the crew were paid off; and theyoung couple — for Kitty was young then — livedvery happily in a lodging-house on South Street,near the docks. This was in New York.

The days flew by like hours, and the stockingin which the little bride kept the funds shrunkand shrunk, until at last there were only three orfour dollars left in the toe of it. Then Kitty wastroubled; for she knew her sailor would have togo to sea again unless he could get employmenton shore. This he endeavored to do, but not withmuch success. One morning as usual he kissedher good day, and set out in search of work.

"Kissed me good-by, and called me his littleIrish lass," sobbed Kitty, telling the story — "kissed me good-by, and, Heaven help me! Iniver set oi on him nor on the likes of him again."

He never came back. Day after day draggedon, night after night, and then the weary weeks.What had become of him ? Had he been mur-dered ? had he fallen into the docks ? had he

—deserted her? No ! she could not believe that; he

was too brave and tender and true. She could notbelieve that. He was dead, dead, or he wouldcome back to her.

Meanwhile the landlord of the lodging-houseturned Kitty into the streets, now that " herman' was gone, and the payment of the rentdoubtful. She got a place as a servant. The fam-ily she lived with shortly moved to Boston, and sheaccompanied them; then they went abroad, butKitty would not leave America. Somehow shedrifted to Rivermouth, and for seven long yearsnever gave speech to her sorrow, until the kind-ness of strangers, who had become friends to her,unsealed the heroic lips.

Kitty's story, you may be sure, made my grand-parents treat her more kindly than ever. In timeshe grew to be regarded less as a servant than asa friend in the home circle, sharing its joys andsorrows — a faithful nurse, a willing slave, a happyspirit in spite of all. I fancy I hear her singingover her work in the kitchen, pausing from timeto time to make some witty reply to Miss Abigail—. for Kitty, like all her race, had a vein of uncon-scious humor. Her bright honest face comes tome out from the past, the light and life of theNutter House when I was a boy at Rivermouth.

CHAPTER VILIGHTS AND SHADOWS

THE first shadow that fell upon me in my newhome was caused by the return of my parents toNew Orleans. Their visit was cut short by busi-ness which required my father's presence inNatchez, where he was establishing a branch ofthe banking-house. When they had gone, a senseof loneliness such as I had never dreamed of filledmy young breast. I crept away to the stable, and,throwing my arms about Gypsy's neck, sobbedaloud. She too had come from the sunny South,and was now a stranger in a strange land.

The little mare seemed to realize our situation,and gave me all the sympathy I could ask, re-peatedly rubbing her soft nose over my face andlapping up my salt tears with evident relish.

When night came, I felt still more lonesome.My grandfather sat in his armchair the greaterpart of the evening, reading the RivermouthBarnacle, the local newspaper. There was no gasin those days, and the Captain read by the aid ofa small block-tin lamp, which he held in one hand.I observed that he had a habit of dropping offinto a doze every three or four minutes, and I for-

Waiting for the Conflagration

got my homesickness at intervals in watching him. Two or three times, to my vast amusement, he scorched the edges of the newspaper with the wick of the lamp ; and at about half past eight o'clock I had the satisfaction — I am sorry to con-fess it was a satisfaction — of seeing the River-mouth Barnacle in flames.

My grandfather leisurely extinguished the fire with his hands, and Miss Abigail, who sat near a low table, knitting by the light of an astral lamp, did not even look up. She was quite used to this catastrophe.

There was little or no conversation during the evening. In fact, I do not remember that anyone spoke at all, excepting once, when the Captain remarked, in a meditative manner, that my parents" must have reached New York by this time ;' at which supposition I nearly strangled myself in at-tempting to intercept a sob.

The monotonous "click click" of Miss Abi-gail's needles made me nervous after a while, and finally drove me out of the sitting-room into the kitchen, where Kitty caused me to laugh by say-ing Miss Abigail thought that what I needed was "a good dose of hot-drops" — a remedy she was forever ready to administer in all emergencies. If a boy broke his leg, or lost his mother, I believe Miss Abigail would have given him hot-drops.

Kitty laid herself out to be entertaining. She told me several funny Irish stones, and

described

some of the odd people living in the town ; but,in the midst of her comicalities, the tears wouldinvoluntarily ooze out of my eyes, though I wasnot a lad much addicted to weeping. Then Kittywould put her arms around me, and tell me not tomind it — that it was not as if I had been left alonein a foreign land with no one to care for me, likea poor girl whom she had once known. I bright-ened up before long, and told Kitty all about theTyphoon and the old seaman, whose name I triedin vain to recall, and was obliged to fall back onplain Sailor Ben.

I was glad when ten o'clock came, the bedtimefor young folks, and old folks too, at the NutterHouse. Alone in the hall-chamber I had my cryout, once for all, moistening the pillow to such anextent that I was obliged to turn it over to finda dry spot to go to sleep on.

My grandfather wisely concluded to put me toschool at once. If I had been permitted to gomooning about the house and stables, I shouldhave kept my discontent alive for months. Thenext morning, accordingly, he took me by thehand, and we set forth for the academy, whichwas located at the farther end of the town.

The Temple School was a two-story brickbuilding, standing in the centre of a great squarepiece of land, surrounded by a high picket fence.There were three or four sickly trees, but no grass,in this inclosure, which had been worn smooth and

S3

hard by the tread of multitudinous feet. I noticedhere and there small holes scooped in the ground,indicating that it was the season for marbles. Abetter playground for base-ball could not have beendevised.

On reaching the schoolhouse door, the Captaininquired for Mr. Grim-shaw. The boy who an-swered our knock ush-ered us into a side room,and in a few minutes —during which my eye tookin forty-two caps hung onforty-two wooden pegs—•Mr. Grimshaw made hisappearance. He was aslender man, with white,fragile hands, and eyesthat glanced half a dozen different ways at once— a habit probably acquired from watching theboys.

After a brief consultation, my grandfather pat-ted me on the head and left me in charge of thisgentleman, who seated himself in front of me andproceeded to sound the depth, or more properlyspeaking, the shallowness, of my attainments. Isuspect that my historical information rather star-tled him. I recollect I gave him to understandthat Richard III. was the last king of England.

This ordeal over, Mr. Grimshaw rose and bade

Mr, Grimshaw

54 THE STORY OF A BAD BOY

me follow him. A door opened, and I stood inthe blaze of forty-two pairs of upturned eyes. Iwas a cool hand for my age, but I lacked theboldness to face this battery without wincing. Ina sort of dazed way I stumbled after Mr. Grimshawdown a narrow aisle between two rows of desks, and shyly took the seat pointed out to me.

The faint buzz that had floated over the school-room at our entrance died away, and the inter-rupted lessons were resumed. By degrees I re-covered my coolness, and ventured to look around me.

The owners of the forty-two caps were seated at small green desks like the one assigned to me. The desks were arranged in six rows, with spaces between just wide enough to prevent the boys' whispering. A blackboard set into the wall ex-tended clear across the end of the room; on a raised platform near the door stood the master's table; and directly in front of this was a recita-tion bench capable of seating fifteen or twenty pupils. A pair of globes, tattooed with dragons and winged horses, occupied a shelf between two windows, which was so high from the floor that nothing but a giraffe could have looked out of them.

Having possessed myself of these details, I scrutinized my new acquaintances with uncon-cealed curiosity, instinctively selecting my friends and picking out my enemies — and in only two cases did I mistake my man.

A sallow boy with bright red hair, sitting in the fourth row, shook his fist at me furtively several times during the morning. I had a presentiment I should have trouble with that boy some day —*a presentiment subsequently realized.

On my left was a chubby little fellow with a great many freckles (this was Pepper Whitcomb), who made some mysterious motions to me. I did not understand them, but, as they were clearly of a pacific nature, I winked my eye at him. This appeared to be satisfactory, for he then went on with his studies. At recess he gave me the core of his apple, though there were several applicants for it.

Presently a boy in a loose olive-green jacket with two rows of brass buttons, held up a folded paper behind his slate, intimating that it was in-tended for me. The paper was passed skillfully from desk to desk until it reached my hands. On opening the scrap, I found that it contained a small piece of molasses candy in an extremely humid state. This was certainly kind. I nodded my acknowledgments and hastily slipped the delicacy into my mouth. In a second I felt my tongue grow red-hot with cayenne pepper.

My face must have assumed a comical expres-sion, for the boy in the olive-green jacket gave an hysterical laugh, for which he was instantly pun-ished by Mr. Grimshaw. I swallowed the fiery candy, though it brought the water to my eyes,

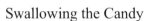

Swallowing the Candy

THE STORY OF A BAD BOY

and managed to look so unconcerned that I was the only pupil in the form who escaped question-ing as to the cause of Marden's misdemeanor.

Marden was his name.

Nothing else occurred that morning to interrupt the ex-ercises, excepting that a boy in the reading class threw us all into convulsions by call-ing Absalom A-bol'-som, —" Abol'som, O my son Abol'-som !" I laughed as loud as any one, but I am not so sure that I should not have pronounced it Abol'som myself.

At recess several of the scholars came to mydesk and shook hands with me, Mr. Grimshawhaving previously introduced me to Phil Adams,charging him to see that I got into no trouble.My new acquaintances suggested that we shouldgo to the playground. We were no sooner out ofdoors than the boy with the red hair thrust his waythrough the crowd and placed himself at my side.

" I say, youngster, if you 're comin' to thisschool you Ve got to toe the mark."

I did not see any mark to toe, and did not un-derstand what he meant; but I replied politely,that, if it was the custom of the school, I shouldbe happy to toe the mark, if he would point it outto me.

"I don't want any of your sarse," said the boy,scowling.

" Look here, Conway!" cried a clear voicefrom the other side of the playground, "you letyoung Bailey alone. He 's a stranger here, andmight be afraid of you, and thrash you. Why doyou always throw yourself in the way of gettingthrashed?"

I turned to the speaker, who by this time hadreached the spot where we stood. Conway slunkoff, favoring me with a parting scowl of defiance.I gave my hand to the boy who had befriendedme — his name was Jack Harris — and thankedhim for his good-will.

" I tell you what it is, Bailey,' he said, return-ing my pressure good-naturedly, " you '11 have tofight Conway before the quarter ends, or you '11have no rest. That fellow is always hankeringafter a licking, and of course you '11 give him oneby and by ; but what's the use of hurrying up anunpleasant job ? Let's have some base-ball. Bythe way, Bailey, you were a good kid not to let ontoGrimshaw about the candy. Charley Mardenwould have caught it twice as heavy. He's sorryhe played the joke on you, and told me to tell youso. Hallo, Blake ! where are the bats ?"

This was addressed to a handsome, frank-lookinglad of about my own age, who was engaged justthen in cutting his initials on the bark of a treenear the schoolhouse. Blake shut up his penknifeand went off to get the bats.

During the game which ensued I made the aoquaintance of Charley Harden, and Binny Wallace,Pepper Whitcomb, Harry Blake, and Fred Lang-don. These boys, none of them more than a yearor two older than I (Binny Wallace was younger),were ever after my chosen comrades. Phil Adamsand Jack Harris were considerably our seniors, andthough they always treated us " kids" very kindly,they generally went with another set. Of course,before long I knew all the Temple boys more orless intimately, but the five I have named were myconstant companions,

My first day at the Temple Grammar School wason the whole satisfactory. I had made severalwarm friends, and only two permanent enemies —Conway and his echo, Seth Rodgers ; for these twoalways went together like a deranged stomach anda headache.

Before the end of the week I had my studieswell in hand. I was a little ashamed at findingmyself at the foot of the various classes, andsecretly determined to deserve promotion. Theschool was an admirable one. I might make thispart of my story more entertaining by picturingMr. Grimshaw as a tyrant with a red nose and alarge stick ; but unfortunately for the purposes ofsensational narrative, Mr. Grimshaw was a quiet,kind-hearted gentleman. Though a rigid disciplin-arian, he had a keen sense of justice, was a goodreader of character, and the boys respected him.

There were two other teachers — a French tutorand a writing-master, who visited the school twicea week. On Wednesdays and Saturdays we weredismissed at noon, and these half-holidays werethe brightest epochs of my existence.

Daily contact with boys who had not beenbrought up as gently as I worked an immediate,and, in some respects, a beneficial change in mycharacter. I had the nonsense taken out of me, as the saying is — some of the nonsense, at least. I became more manly and self-reliant. I discovered that the world was not created exclusively on my account. In New Orleans I labored under the de-lusion that it was. Having neither brother nor sister to give up to at home, and being, moreover, the largest pupil at school there, my will had sel-dom been opposed. At Rivermouth matters were different, and I was not long in adapting myself to the altered circumstances. Of course I got many severe rubs, often unconsciously given ; but I had the sense to see that I was all the better for them.

My social relations with my new schoolfellows were the pleasantest possible. There was always some exciting excursion on foot — a ramble through the pine woods, a visit to the Devil's Pulpit, a high cliff in the neighborhood — or a surreptitious row on the river, involving an exploration of a group of diminutive islands, upon one of which we pitched a tent and played we were the Spanish sailors who

got wrecked there years ago. But the endless pine forest that skirted the town was our favorite haunt. There was a great green pond hidden some-where in its depths, inhabited by a monstrous col-ony of turtles. Harry Blake, who had an eccentric passion for carving his name on everything, never let a captured turtle slip through his fingers with-out leaving his mark engraved on its shell. He must have lettered about two thousand from first to last. We used to call them Harry Blake's sheep.

These turtles were of a discontented and migra-tory turn of mind, and we frequently encountered two or three of them on the cross-roads several miles from their ancestral mud. Unspeakable was our delight whenever we discovered one soberly walking off with Harry Blake's initials ! I have no doubt there are, at this moment, fat ancient tur-tles wandering about that gummy woodland with H. B. neatly cut on their venerable backs.

It soon became a custom among my playmates to make our barn their rendezvous. Gypsy proved a strong attraction. Captain Nutter bought me a little two-wheeled cart, which she drew quite nicely, after kicking out the dasher and breaking the shafts once or twice. With our lunch-baskets and fishing-tackle stowed away under the seat, we used to start off early in the afternoon for the sea-shore, where there were countless marvels in the shape of shells, mosses, and kelp. Gypsy enjoyed the sport as keenly as any of us, even going so far,

one day, as to trot down the beach into the sea where we were bathing. As she took the cart with her, our provisions were not much improved. I shall never forget how squash-pie tastes after being soused in the Atlantic Ocean. Soda-crackers dipped in salt water are palatable, but not squash-pie.

There was a good deal of wet weather during those first six weeks at Rivermouth, and we set ourselves at work to find some in-door amusement for our half - holidays. It was all very well for Amadis de Gaul and Don Quixote not to mind the rain; they had iron overcoats, and were not, from all we can learn, subject to croup and the guidance of their grandfathers. Our case was different.

" Now, boys, what shall we do ?" I asked, ad-dressing a thoughtful conclave of seven, assembled in our barn one dismal rainy afternoon.

" Let's have a theatre," suggested Binny Wal-lace.

The very thing ! But where ? The loft of the stable was ready to burst with hay provided for Gypsy, but the long room over the carriage-house was unoccupied. The place of all places ! My managerial eye saw at a glance its capabilities for a theatre. I had been to the play a great many times in New Orleans, and was wise in matters pertaining to the drama. So here, in due time, was set up some extraordinary scenery of my own painting. The curtain, I recollect, though it worked smoothly enough on other occasions, invariably hitched during the performances ; and itoften required the united energies of the Prince ofDenmark, the King, and the Grave-digger, withan occasional hand from "the fair Ophelia" (Pep-per Whitcomb in a low-necked dress), to hoistthat bit of green cambric.

The theatre, however, was a success, so far as itwent. I retired from the business with no fewerthan fifteen hundred pins, after deducting the head-less, the pointless, and the crooked pins with whichour doorkeeper frequently got " stuck." From firstto last we took in a great deal of this counterfeitmoney. The price of admission to the " River-mouth Theatre " was twenty pins. I played allthe principal parts myself — not that I was a fineractor than the other boys, but because I owned theestablishment.

At the tenth representation, my dramatic careerwas brought to a close by an unfortunate circum-stance. We were playing the drama of " WilliamTell the Hero of Switzerland." Of course I wasWilliam Tell, in spite of Fred Langdon, who wantedto act that character himself. I would not let him,so he withdrew from the company, taking the onlybow and arrow we had. I made a cross-bow outof a piece of whalebone, and did very well withouthim. We had reached that exciting scene whereGessler, the Austrian tyrant, commands Tell toshoot the apple from his son's head. PepperWhitcomb, who played all the juvenile and women

parts, was my son. To guard against mischance,a piece of pasteboard was fastened by a handker-chief over the upper portion of Whitcomb's face,while the arrow to be used was sewed up in astrip of flannel. I was a capital marksman, and

The Drama of William Tell

the big apple, only two yards distant, turned itsrusset cheek fairly towards me.

I can see poor little Pepper now, as he stood with-out flinching, waiting for me to perform my greatfeat. I raised the cross-bow amid the breathlesssilence of the crowded audience— consisting ofseven boys and three girls, exclusive of Kitty Col-lins, who insisted on paying her way in with aclothes-pin. I raised the cross-bow, I repeat.

Twang ! went the whipcord ; but, alas ! instead ofhitting the apple, the arrow flew right into PepperWhitcomb's mouth, which happened to be open atthe time, and destroyed my aim.

I shall never be able to banish that awful mo-ment from my memory. Pepper's roar, expres-sive of astonishment, indignation, and pain, is stillringing in my ears. I looked upon him as a corpse,and, glancing not far into the dreary future, pic-tured myself led forth to execution in the presenceof the very same spectators then assembled.

Luckily poor Pepper was not seriously hurt; butGrandfather Nutter, appearing in the midst of theconfusion (attracted by the howls of young Tell),issued an injunction against all theatricals there-after, and the place was closed ; not, however, with-out a farewell speech from me, in which I said thatthis would have been the proudest moment of mylife if I had not hit Pepper Whitcomb in the mouth.Whereupon the audience (assisted, I am glad tostate, by Pepper) cried " Hear ! hear !' I then at-tributed the accident to Pepper himself, whosemouth, being open at the instant I fired, actedupon the arrow much after the fashion of a whirl-pool, and drew in the fatal shaft. I was about toexplain how a comparatively small maelstrom couldsuck in the largest ship, when the curtain fell ofits own accord, amid the shouts of the audience.

This was my last appearance on any stage. Itwas some time, though, before I heard the end of

the William Tell business. Malicious little boyswho had not been allowed to buy tickets to mytheatre used to cry out after me in the street:

"Who killed Cock Robin ?" I,' said the sparrer,4 With my bow and arrer,I killed Cock Robin ! '"

The sarcasm of this verse was more than I couldstand. And it made Pepper Whitcomb pretty madto be called Cock Robin, I can tell you !

So the days glided on, with fewer clouds andmore sunshine than fall to the lot of most boys.Conway was certainly a cloud. Within school-bounds he seldom ventured to be aggressive ; butwhenever we met about town he never failed tobrush against me, or pull my cap over my eyes,or drive me distracted by inquiring after my fam-ily in New Orleans, always alluding to them ashighly respectable colored people.

Jack Harris was right when he said Conwaywould give me no rest until I fought him. I feltit was ordained ages before our birth that weshould meet on this planet and fight. With theview of not running counter to destiny, I quietlyprepared myself for the impending conflict. Thescene of my dramatic triumphs was turned into agymnasium for this purpose, though I did netopenly avow the fact to the boys. By persistentlystanding on my head, raising heavy weights, andgoing hand over hand up a ladder, I developed my

muscle until my little body was as tough as a hick-ory knot and as supple as tripe. I also took occa-sional lessons in the noble art of self-defense,under the tuition of Phil Adams.

I brooded over the matter until the idea offighting Conway became a part of me. I foughthim in imagination during school-hours ; I dreamedof fighting with him at night, when he would sud-denly expand into a giant twelve feet high, andthen as suddenly shrink into a pygmy so smallthat I could not hit him. In this latter shape hewould get into my hair, or pop into my waistcoat-pocket, treating me with as little ceremony as theLilliputians showed Captain Lemuel Gulliver—allof which was not pleasant, to be sure. On thewhole, Conway was a cloud.

And then I had a cloud at home. It was notGrandfather Nutter, nor Miss Abigail, nor KittyCollins, though they all helped to compose it. Itwas a vague, funereal, impalpable something whichno amount of gymnastic training would enable meto knock over. It was Sunday. If ever I have aboy to bring up in the way he should go, I intendto make Sunday a cheerful day to him. Sundaywas not a cheerful day at the Nutter House. Youshall judge for yourself.

It is Sunday morning. I should premise by say-ing that the deep gloom which has settled overeverything set in like a heavy fog early on Satur-day evening.

At seven o'clock my grandfather comes smile-lessly down stairs. He is dressed in black, andlooks as if he had lost all his friends during thenight. Miss Abigail, also in black, looks as if shewere prepared to bury them, and not indisposed toenjoy the ceremony. Even Kitty Collins hascaught the contagious gloom, as I perceive whenshe brings in the coffee-urn — a solemn and sculp-turesque urn at any time, but monumental now —and sets it down in front of Miss Abigail. MissAbigail gazes at the urn as if it held the ashes ofher ancestors, instead of a generous quantity of fineold Java coffee. The meal progresses in silence.

Our parlor is by no means thrown open everyday. It is open thisJune morning, and ispervaded by a strongsmell of centre-table.The furniture of theroom, and the littleChina ornaments onthe mantel-piece, havea constrained, unfami-liar look. My grand-father sits in a ma-hogany chair, readinga large Bible coveredwith green baize. MissAbigail occupies one end of the sofa, and has herhands crossed stiffly in her lap. I sit in the corner,

Crushed

crushed. Robinson Crusoe and Gil Bias are inclose confinement. Baron Trenck, who managedto escape from the fortress of Glatz, can't for thelife of him get out of our sitting-room closet Eventhe Rivermouth Barnacle is suppressed until Mon-day. Genial converse, harmless books, smiles,lightsome hearts, all are banished. If I want toread anything, I can read Baxter's Saints' Rest.I would die first. So I sit there kicking my heels,thinking about New Orleans, and watching a mor-bid blue-bottle fly that attempts to commit suicideby butting his head against the window-pane.Listen ! — no, yes — it is — it is the robins singingin the garden — the grateful, joyous robins sing-ing away like mad, just as if it were not Sunday.Their audacity tickles me.

My grandfather looks up, and inquires in asepulchral voice if I am ready for Sabbath-school.It is time to go. I like the Sabbath-school; thereare bright young faces there, at all events. WhenI get out into the sunshine alone, I draw a longbreath; I would turn a somersault up againstNeighbor Penhallow's newly painted fence if I hadnot my best trousers on, so glad am I to escapefrom the oppressive atmosphere of the NutterHouse.

Sabbath-school over, I go to meeting, joiningmy grandfather, who does not appear to be anyrelation to me this day, and Miss Abigail, in theporch. Our minister holds out very little hope to

any of us of being saved. Convinced that I am alost creature, in common with the human family,I return home behind my guardians at a snail'space. We have a dead-cold dinner. I saw it laidout yesterday.

There is a long interval between this repast andthe second service, and a still longer interval be-tween the beginning and the end of that service ;for the Rev. Wibird Hawkins's sermons are noneof the shortest, whatever else they may be.

After meeting, my grandfather and I take awalk. We visit, appropriately enough, a neighbor-ing graveyard. I am by this time in a conditionof mind to become a willing inmate of the place.The usual evening prayer-meeting is postponed forsome reason. At half past eight I go to bed.

This is the way Sunday was observed in theNutter House, and pretty generally throughoutthe town, twenty years ago. People who wereprosperous and natural and happy on Saturdaybecame the most rueful of human beings in thebrief space of twelve hours. I do not think therewas any hypocrisy in this. It was merely the oldPuritan austerity cropping out once a week. Manyof these people were pure Christians every day inthe seven — excepting the seventh. Then theywere decorous and solemn to the verge of morose-ness. I should not like to be misunderstood onthis point. Sunday is a blessed day, and there-fore it should not be made a gloomy one. It is

the Lord's day, and I do believe that cheerfulhearts and faces are not unpleasant in His sight.

" O day of rest ? How beautiful, how fair,How welcome to the weary and the old!Day of the Lord! and truce to earthly cares fDay of the Lord, as all our days should be 1Ah, why will man by his austeritiesShut out the blessed sunshine and the light,And make of thee a dungeon of despair !"

CHAPTER VII

ONE MEMORABLE NIGHT

Two months had elapsed since my arrival atRivermouth, when the approach of an importantcelebration produced the greatest excitementamong the juvenile population of the town.

There was very little hard study done in theTemple Grammar School the week preceding theFourth of July. For my part, my heart and brainwere so full of fire-crackers, Roman-candles, rock-ets, pin-wheels, squibs, and gunpowder in variousseductive forms, that I wonder I did not explodeunder Mr. Grimshaw's very nose. I could not doa sum to save me ; I could not tell, for love ormoney, whether Tallahassee was the capital ofTennessee or of Florida; the present and the plu-perfect tenses were inextricably mixed in mymemory, and I did not know a verb from an ad-jective when I met one. This was not alone mycondition, but that of every boy in the school.

Mr. Grimshaw considerately made allowancesfor our temporary distraction, and sought to fixour interest on the lessons by connecting them di-rectly or indirectly with the coming Event. Theclass in arithmetic, for instance, was requested to

state how many boxes of fire-crackers, each boxmeasuring sixteen inches square, could be storedin a room of such and such dimensions. He gaveus the Declaration of Independence for a parsingexercise, and in geography confined his questionsalmost exclusively to localities rendered famous inthe Revolutionary War. " What did the peopleof Boston do with the tea on board the Englishvessels ?" asked our wily instructor.

" Threw it into the river! " shrieked the smallerboys, with an impetuosity that made Mr. Grim-shaw smile in spite of himself. One luckless ur-chin said, " Chucked it," for which happy expres-sion he was kept in at recess.

Notwithstanding these clever stratagems, therewas not much solid work done by anybody. Thetrail of the serpent (an inexpensive but dangerousfire-toy) was over us all. We went round deformedby quantities of Chinese crackers artlessly con-cealed in our trousers-pockets; and if a boy whippedout his handkerchief without proper precaution,he was sure to let off two or three torpedoes.

Even Mr. Grimshaw was made a sort of acces-sory to the universal demoralization. In callingthe school to order, he always rapped on the tablewith a heavy ruler. Under the green baize table-cloth, on the exact spot where he usually struck, acertain boy, whose name I withhold, placed a fattorpedo. The result was a loud explosion, whichcaused Mr. Grimshaw to look queer. Charley

Harden was at the water-pail, at the time, anddirected general attention to himself by stranglingfor several seconds and then squirting a slenderthread of water over the blackboard.

Mr. Grimshaw fixed his eyes reproachfully onCharley, but said no-thing. The real cul-prit (it was not CharleyHarden, but the boywhose name I with-hold) instantly regret-ted his badness, andafter school confessedthe whole thing to Mr.Grimshaw, who heapedcoals of fire upon thenameless boy's head bygiving him five cents forthe Fourth of July. IfMr. Grimshaw had caned this unknown youth, thepunishment would not have been half so severe.

On the last day of June the Captain received aletter from my father, inclosing five dollars "formy son Tom," which enabled that young gentle-man to make regal preparations for the celebrationof our national independence. A portion of thismoney, two dollars, I hastened to invest in fire-works; the balance I put by for contingencies.In placing the fund in my possession, the Captainimposed one condition that dampened my ardor

Mr. Grimshaw looked Queer

considerably — I was to buy no gunpowder. Imight have all the snapping-crackers and torpe-does I wanted; but gunpowder was out of thequestion.

I thought this rather hard, for all my youngfriends were provided with pistols of various sizes.Pepper Whitcomb had a horse-pistol nearly aslarge as himself, and Jack Harris, though he, tobe sure, was a big boy, was going to have a realold-fashioned flint-lock musket. However, I didnot mean to let this drawback destroy my happi-ness. I had one charge of powder stowed awayin the little brass pistol which I brought fromNew Orleans, and was bound to make a noise inthe world once, if I never did again.

It was a custom observed from time immemo-rial for the towns-boys to have a bonfire on theSquare on the midnight before the Fourth. I didnot ask the Captain's leave to attend this cere-mony, for I had a general idea that he would notgive it. If the Captain, I reasoned, does not forbidme, I break no orders by going. Now this was aspecious line of argument, and the mishaps thatbefell me in consequence of adopting it were richlydeserved.

On the evening of the third I retired to bed veryearly, in order to disarm suspicion. I did notsleep a wink, waiting for eleven o'clock to comeround ; and I thought it never would come round,as I lay counting from time to time the slow

strokes of the ponderous bell in the steeple of theOld North Church. At length the laggard hourarrived. While the clock was striking I jumpedout of bed and began dressing.

My grandfather and Miss Abigail were heavysleepers, and I might have stolen downstairs andout at the front door undetected ; but such a com-monplace proceeding did not suit my adventurousdisposition. I fastened one end of a rope (it wasa few yards cut from Kitty Collins's clothes-line)to the bedpost nearest the window, and cautiouslyclimbed out on the wide pediment over the halldoor. I had neglected to knot the rope; the re-sult was, that, the moment I swung clear of thepediment, I descended like a flash of lightning,and warmed both my hands smartly. The rope,moreover, was four or five feet too short; so I gota fall that would have proved serious had I not tumbled into the middle of one of the big rose-bushes growing on either side of the steps.

I scrambled out of that without delay, and was congratulating myself on my good luck, when I saw by the light of the setting moon the form of a man leaning over the garden gate. It was one of the town watch, who had probably been ob-serving my operations with curiosity. Seeing no chance of escape, I put a bold face on the matter and walked directly up to him.

" What on airth air you a-doin' ?" asked the man, grasping the collar of my jacket.

"I live here, sir, if you please," I replied, "and am going to the bonfire. I did n't want to wake up the old folks, that's all."

The man cocked his eye at me in the most amiable manner, and released his hold. c

"Boys is boys," he muttered. He did not attempt to stop me as I slipped through the gate, i

Once beyond his clutches, I took to my heels and soon reached the Square, where I found forty or fifty fellows assembled, engaged in building a pyramid of tar-barrels. The palms of my hands still tingled so that I could not join in the sport. I stood in the doorway of the Nautilus Bank, watching the workers, among whom I recognized lots of my schoolmates. They looked like a legion of imps, coming and going in the twilight, busy in raising some infernal edifice. What a Babel of voices it was, everybody directing everybody else, and everybody doing everything wrong !

When all was prepared, some one applied a match to the sombre pile. A fiery tongue thrust itself out here and there, then suddenly the whole fabric burst into flames, blazing and crackling beautifully. This was a signal for the boys to join hands and dance around the burning barrels, which they did, shouting like mad creatures. When the fire had burnt down a little, fresh staves were brought and heaped on the pyre. In the excitement of the moment I forgot my tingling palms, and found myself in the thick of the ca-rousal.

Before we were half ready, our combustible material was expended, and a disheartening kind of darkness settled down upon us. The boys col-lected together here and there in knots, consulting as to what should be done. It yet lacked four or five hours of daybreak, and none of us were in the humor to return to bed. I approached one of the groups standing near the town-pump, and discov-ered in the uncertain light of the dying brands the figures of Jack Harris, Phil Adams, Harry Blake, and Pepper Whitcomb, their faces streaked with perspiration and tar, and their whole appearance suggestive of New Zealand chiefs.

" Hullo ! here's Tom Bailey !' shouted Pepper Whitcomb; "he'll join in!"

Of course he would. The sting had gone out of my hands, and I was ripe for anything — none the less ripe for not knowing what was on the tapis. After whispering together for a moment, the boys motioned me to follow them.

We glided out from the crowd and silently wended our way through a neighboring alley, at the head of which stood a tumble-down old barn, owned by one Ezra Wingate. In former days this was the stable of the mail-coach that ran between Rivermouth and Boston. When the railroad super-seded that primitive mode of travel, the lumbering vehicle was rolled into the barn, and there it stayed. The stage-driver, after prophesying the immediate downfall of the nation, died of grief and apoplexy,

and the old coach followed in his wake as fast as it could by quietly dropping to pieces. The barn had the reputation of being haunted, and I think we all kept very close together when we found ourselves standing in the black shadow cast by the tall gable. Here, in a low voice, Jack Harris laid bare his plan, which was to burn the ancient stage-coach.

" The old trundle-cart is n't worth twenty-five cents," said Jack Harris, " and Ezra Wingate ought to thank us for getting the rubbish out of the way. But if any fellow here does n't want to havea hand in it, let him cut and run, and keep a quiettongue in his head ever after."

With this he pulled out the staples that held therusty padlock, and the big barn door swung slowlyopen. The interior of the stable was pitch-dark,of course. As we made a movement to enter, asudden scrambling, and the sound of heavy bodiesleaping in all directions, caused us to start back interror.

" Rats ! " cried Phil Adams.

" Bats !" exclaimed Harry Blake.

" Cats!M suggested Jack Harris. " Who'safraid ? "

Well, the truth is, we were all afraid ; and if thepole of the stage had not been lying close to thethreshold, I do not believe anything on earth wouldhave induced us to cross it. We seized hold ofthe pole-straps and succeeded with great trouble

in dragging the coach out. The two fore wheelshad rusted to the axle-tree, and refused to revolve.It was the merest skeleton of a coach. The cush-ions had long since been removed, and the leatherhangings, where they had not crumbled away, dan-gled in shreds from the worm-eaten frame. A loadof ghosts and a span of phantom horses to dragthem would have made the ghastly thing complete.

Luckily for our undertaking, the stable stood atthe top of a very steep hill. With three boys topush behind, and two in front to steer, we startedthe old coach on its last trip with little or no diffi-culty. Our speed increased every moment, and,the fore wheels becoming unlocked as we arrivedat the foot of the declivity, we charged upon thecrowd like a regiment of cavalry, scattering thepeople right and left. Before reaching the bonfire,to which some one had added several bushels ofshavings, Jack Harris and Phil Adams, who weresteering, dropped on the ground, and allowed thevehicle to pass over them, which it did withoutinjuring them; but the boys who were clinging fordear life to the trunk-rack behind fell over theprostrate steersmen, and there we all lay in a heap,two or three of us quite picturesque with the nose-bleed.

The coach, with an intuitive perception of whatwas expected of it, plunged into the centre ofthe kindling shavings, and stopped. The flamessprung up and clung to the rotten woodwork, which

burned like tinder. At this moment a figure wasseen leaping wildly from the inside of the blazingcoach. The figure made three bounds towards us,and tripped over Harry Blake. It was PepperWhitcomb, with his hair somewhat singed, andhis eyebrows completely scorched off!

Pepper had slyly ensconced himself on the backseat before we started, intending to have a neatlittle ride down hill, and a laugh at us afterwards.But the laugh, as it happened, was on our side, orwould have been, if half a dozen watchmen hadnot suddenly pounced down upon us, as we layscrambling on the ground, weak with mirth overPepper's misfortune. We were collared andmarched off before we well knew what had hap-pened.

The abrupt transition from the noise and lightof the Square to the silent, gloomy brick room inthe rear of the Meat Market seemed like the workof enchantment. We stared at each other aghast.

" Well," remarked Jack Harris, with a sickly smile," this is a go !'

" No go, I should say," whimpered Harry Blake,glancing at the bare brick walls and the heavyiron-plated door.

" Never say die," muttered Phil Adams, dolefully.

The bridewell was a small low-studded chamberbuilt up against the rear end of the Meat Market,and approached from the Square by a narrow pas-sageway. A portion of the room was

partitioned

The Interrupted Celebration

off into eight cells, numbered, each capable of hold-ing two persons. The cells were full at the time, as we presently discovered by seeing several hid-eous faces leering out at us through the gratings of the doors.

A smoky oil-lamp in a lantern suspended from the ceiling threw a flickering light over the apart-ment, which contained no furniture excepting a couple of stout wooden benches. It was a dismal place by night, and only little less dismal by day, for the tall houses surrounding " the lock-up " pre-vented the faintest ray of sunshine from penetrat-ing the ventilator over the door— a long narrow window opening inward and propped up by a piece of lath.

As we seated ourselves in a row on one of the benches, I imagine that our aspect was anything but cheerful. Adams and Harris looked very anx-ious, and Harry Blake, whose nose had just stopped bleeding, was mournfully carving his name, by sheer force of habit, on the prison bench. I do not think I ever saw a more " wrecked " expression on any human countenance than Pepper Whitcomb's pre-sented. His look of natural astonishment at find-ing himself incarcerated in a jail was considerably heightened by his lack of eyebrows.

As for me, it was only by thinking how the lateBaron Trenck would have conducted himself undersimilar circumstances that I was able to restrainmy tears.

None of us were inclined to conversation. Adeep silence, broken now and then by a startlingsnore from the cells, reigned throughout the cham-ber. By and by Pepper Whitcomb glanced ner-vously towards Phil Adams and said, " Phil, do youthink they will — hang us f"

" Hang your grandmother!' returned Adams, jimpatiently; "what I'm afraid of is that they'llkeep us locked up until the Fourth is over."

" You ain't smart ef they do!' cried a voicefrom one of the cells. It was a deep bass voicethat sent a chill through me.

" Who are you ? " said Jack Harris, addressingthe cells in general; for the echoing qualities ofthe room made it difficult to locate the voice.

"That don't matter," replied the speaker, put-ting his face close up to the gratings of No. 3," but ef I was a youngster like you, free an' easyoutside there, this spot would n't hold me long."

" That 's so!" chimed several of the prison-birds, wagging their heads behind the iron lat-tices.

" Hush !' whispered Jack Harris, rising fromhis seat and walking on tip-toe to the door of cellNo. 3. "What would you do ?"

" Do ? Why, I 'd pile them 'ere benches up aginthat 'ere door, an' crawl out of that 'ere windcr inno time. That's my adwice."

"And werry good adwice it is, Jim," said theoccupant of No. 5 approvingly.

Jack Harris seemed to be of the same opinion,for he hastily placed the benches one on the topof another under the ventilator, and, climbing upon the highest bench,peeped out into thepassageway.

"If any gent hap-pens to have a nine-pence about him," saidthe man in cell No.3, " there 's a sufferin'family here as couldmake use of it. Small-est favors gratefullyreceived, an* no ques-tions axed."

This appeal toucheda new silver quarterof a dollar in my trou-sers-pocket ; I fishedout the coin from amass of fireworks, and

. . " What-wouldyou do ?gave it to the prisoner.

He appeared to be so good-natured a fellow that

I ventured to ask what he had done to get into jail.

" Intirely innocent. I was clapped in here by arascally nevew as wishes to enjoy my wealth aforeI 'm dead."

" Your name, sir ?" I inquired, with a view of

reporting the outrage to my grandfatrier and hav-ing the injured person reinstated in society.

" Git out, you insolent young reptyle ! " shoutedthe man, in a passion.

I retreated precipitately, amid a roar of laughterfrom the other cells.

" Can't you keep still ? " exclaimed Harris, with-drawing his head from the window.

A portly watchman usually sat on a stool out-side the door day and night; but on this particularoccasion, his services being required elsewhere,the bridewell had been left to guard itself.

" All clear," whispered Jack Harris, as he van-ished through the aperture and dropped softly onthe ground outside. We all followed him expe-ditiously — Pepper Whitcomb and myself gettingstuck in the window for a moment in our franticefforts not to be last.

"Now, boys, everybody for himself!"

CHAPTER VIII

THE ADVENTURES OF A FOURTH

THE sun cast a broad column of quivering goldacross the river at the foot of our street, just as Ireached the doorstep of the Nutter House. KittyCollins, with her dress tucked about her so thatshe looked as if she had on a pair of calico trou-sers, was washing off the sidewalk.

" Arrah, you bad boy ! " cried Kitty, leaning onthe mop-handle, "the Capen has jist been askin'for you. He's gone up town, now. It's a natething you done with my clothes-line, and it's meyou may thank for gettin' it out of the way beforethe Capen come down."

The kind creature had hauled in the rope, andmy escapade had not been discovered by the fam-ily ; but I knew very well that the burning of thestage-coach, and the arrest of the boys concernedin the mischief, were sure to reach my grandfather'sears sooner or later.

" Well, Thomas," said the old gentleman, an houror so afterwards, beaming upon me benevolentlyacross the breakfast-table, " you did n't wait to becalled this morning."

"No, sir," I replied, growing very warm, "I
took a little run up town to see what was going on.'

I did not say anything about the little run I tookhome again !

" They had quite a time on the Square last night,"remarked Captain Nutter, looking up from theRivermouth Barnacle, which was always placed be-side his coffee-cup at breakfast.

I felt that my hair was preparing to stand on end."Quitc a time," continued my grandfather." Some boys broke into Ezra Wingate's barn andcarried off the old stage-coach. The young ras-cals ! I do believe they 'd burn up the whole townif they had their way."

With this he resumed the paper. After a longsilence he exclaimed, "Hullo!" — upon which Inearly fell off the chair.

"' Miscreants unknown/ " read my grandfather, following the paragraphwith his forefinger; "' es-caped from the bridewell,leaving no clew to theiridentity, except the letterH, cut on one of thebenches/ ' Five dollarsi« Miscreants unknown* reward offered for the ap-prehension of the perpe-trators.' Sho! I hope Wingate will catch them."I do not see how I continued to live, for on hear-ing this the breath went entirely out of my body.

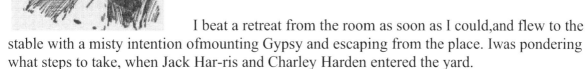

I beat a retreat from the room as soon as I could,and flew to the stable with a misty intention ofmounting Gypsy and escaping from the place. Iwas pondering what steps to take, when Jack Har-ris and Charley Harden entered the yard.

"I say," said Harris as blithe as a lark, "hasold Wingate been here ?"

" Been here ? " I cried, " I should hope not!"

" The whole thing's out, you know," said Harris,pulling Gypsy's forelock over her eyes and blowingplayfully into her nostrils.

" You don't mean it!" I gasped.

" Yes, I do, and we are to pay Wingate threedollars apiece. He'll make rather a good spec outof it."

" But how did he discover that we were the —the miscreants ?" I asked, quoting mechanicallyfrom the Rivermouth Barnacle.

" Why, he saw us take the old ark, confoundhim ! He 's been trying to sell it any time theseten years. Now he has sold it to us. When hefound that we had slipped out of the Meat Market,he went right off and wrote the advertisementoffering five dollars reward ; though he knew wellenough who had taken the coach, for he cameround to my father's house before the paper wasprinted to talk the matter over. Was n't the gov-ernor mad, though ! But it's all settled, I tell you.We 're to pay Wingate fifteen dollars for the oldgo-cart, which he wanted to sell the other day for seventy-five cents, and could n't. It's a down-right swindle. But the funny part of it is to come."

" Oh, there's a funny part to it, is there ?" Iremarked bitterly.

" Yes. The moment Bill Conway saw the adver-tisement, he knew it was Harry Blake who cut thatletter H on the bench ; so off he rushes up to Win-gate — kind of him, was n't it ? — and claims thereward. ' Too late, young man,' says old Wingate,'the culprits has been discovered.' You see Sly-boots had n't any intention of paying that five dol-lars."

Jack Harris's statement lifted a weight frommy bosom. The article in the Rivermouth Barna-cle had placed the affair before me in a new light.I had thoughtlessly committed a grave offense.Though the property in question was valueless, wewere clearly wrong in destroying it. At the sametime, Mr. Wingate had tacitly sanctioned the actby not preventing it when he might easily have doneso. He had allowed his property to be destroyedin order that he might realize a large profit.

Without waiting to hear more, I went straightto Captain Nutter, and, laying my remaining threedollars on his knee, confessed my share in the pre-vious night's transaction.

The Captain heard me through in profound silence,pocketed the bank-notes, and walked off withoutspeaking a word. He had punished me in his ownwhimsical fashion at the breakfast-table, for, at the

very moment he was harrowing up my soul by read-ing the extracts from the Rivermouth Barnacle, henot only knew all about the bonfire, but had paidEzra Wingate his three dollars. Such was the du-plicity of that aged impostor !

I think Captain Nutter was justified in retainingmy pocket-money, as additional punishment, thoughthe possession of it later in the day would have gotme out of a difficult position, as the reader will seefarther on.

I returned with a light heart and a large piece ofpunk to my friends in the stable-yard, where we cele-brated the termination of our trouble by setting offtwo packs of fire-crackers in an empty wine-cask.They made a prodigious racket, but failed somehowto fully express my feelings. The little brass pistolin my bedroom suddenly occurred to me. It hadbeen loaded I do not know how many months, longbefore I left New Orleans, and now was the time,if ever, to fire it off. Muskets, blunderbusses, andpistols were banging away lively all over town,and the smell of gunpowder, floating on the air, setme wild to add something respectable to the uni-versal din.

When the pistol was produced, Jack Harris ex-amined the rusty cap and prophesied that it would -not explode.

" Never mind," said I, " let's try it."

I had fired the pistol once, secretly, in New Or-leans, and, remembering the noise it gave birth to

on that occasion, I shut both eyes tight as I pulledthe trigger. The hammer clicked on the cap witha dull, dead sound. Then Harris tried it; thenCharley Harden; then I took it again, and afterthree or four trials was on the point of giving it

"Art you hurt?"

up as a bad job, when the obstinate thing went offwith a tremendous explosion, nearly jerking my armfrom the socket. The smoke cleared away, andthere I stood with the stock of the pistol clutchedconvulsively in my hand — the barrel, lock, trigger,and ramrod having vanished into thin air.

"Are you hurt? " cried the boys in one breath.

" N—no," I replied, dubiously, for the concussionhad bewildered me a little.

When I realized the nature of the calamity, mygrief was excessive. I cannot imagine what ledme to do so ridiculous a thing, but I gravely bur-ied the remains of my beloved pistol in our backgarden, and erected over the mound a slate tabletto the effect that " Mr. Barker, formerly of NewOrleans, was Killed accidently on the Fourth ofJuly, 18— in the 2d year of his Age."1 BinnyWallace, arriving on the spot just after the disaster,and Charley Harden (who enjoyed the obsequiesimmensely), acted with me as chief mourners. I,for my part, was a very sincere one.

As I turned away in a disconsolate mood fromthe garden, Charley Harden remarked that heshould not be surprised if the pistol-but took rootand grew into a mahogany-tree or something. Hesaid he once planted an old musket-stock, andshortly afterwards a lot of shoots sprung up ! JackHarris laughed ; but neither I nor Binny Wallacesaw Charley's wicked joke.

We were now joined by Pepper Whitcomb, FredLangdon, and several other desperate characters,on their way to the Square, which was always abusy place when public festivities were going on.Feeling that I was still in disgrace with the Cap-

1 This inscription is copied from a triangular-shaped piece ofslate, still preserved in the garret of the Nutter House, togetherwith the pistol-but itself, which was subsequently dug up for a.post-mortem examination.

94 THE STORY OF A BAD BOY

tain, I thought it politic to ask his consent beforeaccompanying the boys.

He gave it with some hesitation, advising meto be careful not to get in front of the firearms.Once he put his fingers mechanically into his vest-pocket and half drew forth some dollar-bills, thenslowly thrust them back again as his sense of justiceovercame his genial disposition. I guess it cut theold gentleman to the heart to be obliged to keepme out of my pocket-money. I know it did me.However, as I was passing through the hall, MissAbigail, with a very severe cast of countenance,slipped a brand-new quarter into my hand. Wehad silver currency in those days, thank Heaven!

Great were the bustle and confusion on theSquare. By the way, I don't know why theycalled this large open space a square, unless be-cause it was an oval —an oval formed by the con-fluence of half a dozen streets, now thronged bycrowds of smartly dressed towns-people and coun-try folks ; for Rivermouth on the Fourth was thecentre of attraction to the inhabitants of theneighboring villages.

On one side of the Square were twenty or thirtybooths arranged in a semicircle, gay with littleflags and seductive with lemonade, ginger-beer,and seed cakes. Here and there were tables atwhich could be purchased the smaller sort of fire-works, such as pin-wheels, serpents, double-head-ers, and punk warranted not to go out. Many of the adjacent houses made a pretty display of bunt-ing, and across each of the streets opening on theSquare was an arch of spruce and evergreen, blos-soming all over with patriotic mottoes and paperroses.

It was a noisy, merry, bewildering scene as wecame upon the ground. The incessant rattle ofsmall arms, the booming of the twelve-pounderfiring on the Mill Dam, and the silvery clangor ofthe church-bells ringing simultaneously — not tomention an ambitious brass-band that was blow-ing itself to pieces on a balcony — were enough todrive one distracted. We amused ourselves for anhour or two, darting in and out among the crowdand setting off our crackers. At one o'clock theHon. Hezekiah Elkins mounted a platform in themiddle of the Square and delivered an oration, towhich his " feller-citizens" did not pay much atten-tion, having all they could do to dodge the squibsthat were set loose upon them by mischievous boysstationed on the surrounding housetops.

Our little party, which had picked up recruitshere and there, not being swayed by eloquence,withdrew to a booth on the outskirts of the crowd,where we regaled ourselves with root beer at twocents a glass. I recollect being much struck bythe placard surmounting this tent:

ROOT BEERSOLD HERE.

It seemed to me the perfection of pith and poetry,

THE STORY OF A BAD BOY

The Perfection of Pith and Poetry

What could be more terse ? Not a word to spare,and yet everything fully expressed. Rhyme andrhythm faultless. It was a delightful poet whomade those verses. As for the beer itself — that,I think, must have been made from the root of all

evil! A single glassof it insured an un-interrupted pain fortwenty-four hours.

The influence ofmy liberality workingon Charley Harden— for it was I whopaid for the beer —he presently invitedus all to take an ice-cream with him at Pettingil'ssaloon. Pettingil was the Delmonico of River-mouth. He furnished ices and confectionery foraristocratic balls and parties, and did not disdainto officiate as leader of the orchestra at the same ;for Pettingil played on the violin, as Pepper Whit-comb described it, " like Old Scratch."

Pettingil's confectionery store was on the cor-ner of Willow and High streets. The saloon, sep-arated from the shop by a flight of three stepsleading to a door hung with faded red drapery,had about it an air of mystery and seclusion quitedelightful. Four windows, also draped, faced theside - street, affording an unobstructed view ofMarm Hatch's back yard, where a number of inex-

plicable garments on a clothes-line were always tobe seen careering in the wind.

There was a lull just then in the ice-cream busi-ness, it being dinner-time, and we found the sa-loon unoccupied. When we had seated ourselvesaround the largest marble-topped table, CharleyHarden in a manly voice ordered twelve sixpennyice-creams, " strawberry and verneller mixed."

It was a magnificent sight, those twelve chillyglasses entering the room on a waiter, the red andwhite custard rising from each glass like a church-steeple, and the spoon-handle shooting up fromthe apex like a spire. I doubt if a person of thenicest palate could have distinguished, with hiseyes shut, which was the vanilla and which thestrawberry: but if I could at this moment obtaina cream tasting as that did, I would give five dol-lars for a very small quantity.

We fell to with a will, and so evenly balancedwere our capabilities that we finished our creamstogether, the spoons clinking in the glasses likeone spoon.

" Let's have some more !" cried Charley Mar-den, with the air of Aladdin ordering up a freshhogshead of pearls and rubies. " Tom Bailey, tellPettingil to send in another round."

Could I credit my ears ? I looked at him to seeif he were in earnest. He meant it. In a momentmore I was leaning over the counter giving direc-tions for a second supply. Thinking it would make

no difference to such a gorgeous young sybarite asMarden, I took the liberty of ordering ninepennycreams this time.

On returning to the saloon, what was my horrorat finding it empty !

There were the twelve cloudy glasses, standingin a circle on the sticky marble slab, and not a boyto be seen. A pair of hands letting go their holdon the window-sill outside explained matters. Ihad been made a victim.

I could n't stay and face Pettingil, whose pep-pery temper was well known among the boys. Ihad not a cent in the world to appease him. Whatshould I do? I heard the clink of approachingglasses — the ninepenny creams. I rushed to thenearest window. It was only five feet to theground. I threw myself out as if I had been anold hat.

Landing on my feet, I fled breathlessly downHigh Street, through Willow, and was turning intoBrierwood Place when the sound of several voices,calling to me in distress, stopped my progress.

" Look out, you fool! the mine ! the mine !"yelled the warning voices.

Several men and boys were standing at the headof the street, making insane gestures to me toavoid something. But I saw no mine, only in themiddle of the road in front of me was a commonflour-barrel, which, as I gazed at it, suddenly roseinto the air with a terrific explosion. I felt myself

THE ADVENTURES OF A FOURTH

99

thrown violently off my feet. I remember nothingelse, excepting that, as I went up, I caught a mo-mentary glimpse of Ezra Wingate leering throughhis shop window like an avenging spirit.

The mine that had wrought me woe was not prop-erly a mine at all, but merely a few ounces of pow-der placed under an empty keg or barrel and firedwith a slow-match. Boys who did not happen to

The Result of the Explosion

have pistols or cannon generally burnt their pow-der in this fashion.

For an account of what followed I am indebted tohearsay, for I was insensible when the bystanderspicked me up and carried me home on a shutterborrowed from the proprietor of Pettingil's saloon.I was supposed to be killed, but happily (happilyfor me at least) I was merely stunned. I lay in asemi-unconscious state until eight o'clock that

night, when I attempted to speak. Miss Abigail,who watched by the bedside, put her ear down tomy lips and was saluted with these remarkablewords :

" Strawberry and verneller mixed !I!

" Mercy on us ! what is the boy saying ? " criedMiss Abigail.

" ROOTBEERSOLDHERE ! "

CHAPTER IX

I BECOME AN R. M. C.

IN the course of ten days I recovered sufficientlyfrom my injuries to attend school, where, for a littlewhile, I was looked upon as a hero, on account ofhaving been blown up. What do we not make ahero of ? The distraction which prevailed in theclasses the week preceding the Fourth had sub-sided, and nothing remained to indicate the recentfestivities, excepting a noticeable want of eyebrowson the part of Pepper Whitcomb and myself.

In August we had two weeks' vacation. It wasabout this time that I became a member of theRivermouth Centipedes, a secret society composedof twelve of the Temple Grammar School boys.This was an honor to which I had long aspired,but, being a new boy, I was not admitted to thefraternity until my character had fully developeditself.

It was a very select society, the object of whichI never fathomed, though I was an active memberof the body during the remainder of my residenceat Rivermouth, and at one time held the onerousposition of F. C. — First Centipede. Each of theelect wore a copper cent (some occult association

being established between a cent apiece and a cen-tipede !) suspended by a string round his neck.The medals were worn next the skin, and it waswhile bathing one day at Grave Point, with JackHarris and Fred Langdon, that I had my curiosityroused to the highest pitch by a sight of thesesingular emblems. As soon as I ascertained theexistence of a boys' club, of course I was readyto die to join it. And eventually I was allowed tojoin.

The initiation ceremony took place in Fred Lang-don's barn, where I was submitted to a series oftrials not calculated to soothe the nerves of a tim-orous boy. Before being led to the Grotto of En-chantment— such was the modest title given tothe loft over my friend's wood-house — my handswere securely pinioned, and my eyes covered witha thick silk handkerchief. At the head of the stairsI was told in an unrecognizable, husky voice, thatit was not yet too late to retreat if I felt myselfphysically too weak to undergo the necessary tor-tures. I replied that I was not too weak, in a tonewhich I intended to be resolute, but which, in spiteof me, seemed to come from the pit of my stomach.

" It is well! " said the husky voice.

I did not feel so sure about that ; but, havingmade up my mind to be a Centipede, a Centipede Iwas bound to be. Other boys had passed throughthe ordeal and lived, why should not I ?

A prolonged silence followed this preliminary ex-

animation, and I was wondering what would comenext, when a pistol fired off close by my ear deaf-ened me for a moment. The unknown voice thendirected me to take ten steps forward and stop atthe word halt. I took ten steps, and halted.

" Stricken mortal," said a second husky voice,more husky, if possible, than the first, "if you hadadvanced another inch, you would have disap-peared down an abyss three thousand feet deep!'

I naturally shrunk back at this friendly piece ofinformation. A prick from some two-pronged in-strument, evidently a pitchfork, gently checked myretreat. I was then conducted to the brink of sev-eral other precipices, andordered to step over manydangerous chasms, wherethe result would have beeninstant death if I had com-mitted the least mistake.I have neglected to saythat my movements wereaccompanied by dismalgroans from different partsof the grotto.

Finally, I was led up a steep plank to what ap-peared to me an incalcula-ble height. Here I stood breathless while the by-laws were read aloud. A more extraordinary code of laws never came from the brain of man. The

Gently checked

penalties attached to the abject being who should reveal any of the secrets of the society were enough to make the blood run cold. A second pistol-shot was heard, the something I stood on sunk with a crash beneath my feet, and I fell two miles, as nearly as I could compute it. At the same instant the handkerchief was whisked from my eyes, and I found myself standing in an empty hogshead surrounded by twelve masked figures fantastically dressed. One of the conspirators was really ap-palling with a tin sauce-pan on his head, and a tiger-skin sleigh-robe thrown over his shoulders. I scarcely need say that there were no vestiges to be seen of the fearful gulfs over which I had passed so cautiously. My ascent had been to the top of the hogshead, and my descent to the bottom thereof. Holding one another by the hand, and chanting a low dirge, the Mystic Twelve revolved about me. This concluded the ceremony. With a merry shout the boys threw off their masks, and I was declared a regularly installed member of the R. M. C.

I afterwards had a good deal of sport out of the club, for these initiations, as you may imagine, were sometimes very comical spectacles, especially when the aspirant for centipedal honors happened to be of a timid disposition. If he showed the slightest terror, he was certain to be tricked unmercifully. One of our subsequent devices — a humble inven-tion of my own — was to request the blindfolded

candidate to put out his tongue, whereupon the First Centipede would say, in a low tone, as if not intended for the ear of the victim, " Diabolus, fetch me the red-hot iron ! " The expedition with which that tongue would disappear was simply ridic-ulous.

Our meetings were held in various barns, at no stated periods, but as circumstances suggested. Any member had a right to call a meeting. Each boy who failed to report himself was fined one cent. Whenever a member had reasons for thinking that another member would be unable to attend, he called a meeting. For instance, immediately on learning the death of Harry Blake's great-grand-father, I issued a call. By these simple and ingen-ious measures we kept our treasury in a flourish-ing condition, sometimes having on hand as much as a dollar and a quarter.

I have said that the society had no especial ob-ject. It is true, there was a tacit understanding among us that the Centipedes were to stand by one another on all occasions, though I don't remember that they did ; but further than this we had no purpose, unless it was to accomplish as a body the same amount of mischief which we were sure to do as individuals. To mystify the staid and slow-going Rivermouthians was our frequent pleasure. Several of our pranks won us such a reputationamong the townsfolk that we were credited withhaving a large finger in whatever went amiss inthe place.

One morning, about a week after my admissioninto the secret order, the quiet citizens awoke tofind that the sign-boards of all the principal streetshad changed places during the night. People whowent trustfully to sleep in Currant Square openedtheir eyes in Honeysuckle Terrace. Jones's Av-enue at the north end had suddenly become Wal-nut Street, and Peanut Street was nowhere to befound. Confusion reigned. The town authoritiestook the matter in hand without delay, and six ofthe Temple Grammar School boys were summonedto appear before Justice Clapham.

Having tearfully disclaimed to my grandfatherall knowledge of the transaction, I disappearedfrom the family circle, and was not apprehendeduntil late in the afternoon, when the Captaindragged me ignominiously from the haymow andconducted me, more dead than alive, to the officeof Justice Clapham. Here I encountered fiveother pallid culprits, who had been fished out ofdivers coal-bins, garrets, and chicken-coops, to an-swer the demands of the outraged laws. (CharleyMarden had hidden himself in a pile of gravel be-hind his father's house, and looked like a recentlyexhumed mummy.)

There was not the least evidence against us;and indeed we were wholly innocent of the offense.The trick, as was afterwards proved, had beenplayed by a party of soldiers stationed at the fortin the harbor. We were indebted for our arrest

The Initiation

to Master Conway, who had slyly dropped a hint, within the hearing of Selectman Mudge, to the effect that "young Bailey and his five cronies could tell something about them signs." When he was called upon to make good his assertion, he was

Charley Marden exhumed considerably more terrified than the Centipedes, though they were ready to sink into their shoes.

At our next meeting it was unanimously resolved that Conway's animosity should not be quietly sub-mitted to. He had sought to inform against us in the stage-coach business; he had volunteered to carry Pettingil's " little bill" for twenty-four ice-creams to Charley Marden's father; and now he had caused us to be arraigned before Justice Clap-

ham on a charge equally groundless and painful After much noisy discussion a plan of retaliation was agreed upon.

There was a certain slim, mild apothecary in the town, by the name of Meeks. It was generally given out that Mr. Meeks had a vague desire to get married, but, being a shy and timorous youth, lacked the moral courage to do so. It was also well known that the Widow Conway had not buried her heart with the late lamented. As to her shyness, that was not so clear. Indeed, her attentions to Mr. Meeks, whose mother she might have been, were of a nature not to be misunder-stood, and were not misunderstood by any one but Mr. Meeks himself.

The widow carried on a dressmaking establish-ment at her residence on the corner opposite Meeks's drug-store, and kept a wary eye on all the young ladies from Miss Dorothy Gibbs's Fe-male Institute who patronized the shop for soda-water, acid-drops, and slate-pencils. In the after-noon the widow was usually seen seated, smartly dressed, at her window upstairs, casting destruc-tive glances across the street — the artificial roses in her cap and her whole languishing manner say-ing as plainly as a label on a prescription, " To be Taken Immediately!" But Mr. Meeks did n't take.

The lady's fondness and the gentleman's blind-ness were topics ably handled at every sewing-cir-cle in the town. It was through these two luck-

less individuals that we proposed to strike a blow at the common enemy. To kill less than three birds with one stone did not suit our sanguinary purpose. We disliked the widow not so much for her sentimentality as for being the mother of Bill Conway; we disliked Mr. Meeks, not because he was insipid, like his own syrups, but because the widow loved him; Bill Conway we hated for him-self.

Late one dark Saturday night in September we carried our plan into effect. On the following morning, as the orderly citizens wended their way to church past the widow's abode, their sober facesrelaxed at beholding over her front door the well-known gilt Mortar and Pestle which usually stoodon the top of a pole on the opposite corner; whilethe passers on that side of the street were equallyamused and scandalized at seeing a placard bear-ing the following announcement tacked to thedruggist's window-shutters:

The naughty cleverness of the joke (which Ishould be sorry to defend) was recognized at once.It spread like wildfire over the town, and, thoughthe mortar and placard were speedily removed, ourtriumph was complete. The whole communitywas on the broad grin, and our participation inthe affair seemingly unsuspected.

It was those wicked soldiers at the fort!

CHAPTER X

I FIGHT CONWAY

THERE was one person, however, who cherisheda strong suspicion that the Centipedes had had ahand in the business; and that person was Con-way. His red hair seemed to change to a livelierred, and his sallow cheeks to a deeper sallow, aswe glanced at him stealthily over the tops of ourslates the next day in school. He knew wewere watching him, and made sundry mouths andscowled in the most threatening way over hissums.

Conway had an accomplishment peculiarly hisown — that of throwing his thumbs out of joint atwill. Sometimes while absorbed in study, or onbecoming nervous at recitation, he performed thefeat unconsciously. Throughout this entire morn-ing his thumbs were observed to be in a chronicstate of dislocation, indicating great mental agita-tion on the part of the owner. We fully expectedan outbreak from him at recess; but the inter-mission passed off tranquilly, somewhat to our dis-appointment.

At the close of the afternoon session it hap-pened that Binny Wallace and myself, having got

swamped in our Latin exercise, were detained inschool for the purpose of refreshing our memorieswith a page of Mr. Andrews's perplexing irregularverbs. Binny Wallace finishing his task first, wasdismissed. I followed shortly after, and, on step-ping into the playground, saw my little friendplastered, as it were, up against the fence, andConway standing in front of him ready to delivera blow on the upturned, unprotected face, whosegentleness would have stayed any arm but a cow-ard's.

Seth Rodgers, with both hands in his pockets,was leaning against the pump lazily enjoying thesport; but on seeing me sweep across the yard,whirling my strap of books in the air like a sling,he called out lustily, " Lay low, Conway! here 'syoung Bailey!"

Conway turned just in time to catch on hisshoulder the blow intended for his head. Hereached forward one of his long arms — he hadarms like a windmill, that boy — and, grasping meby the hair, tore out quite a respectable handful.The tears flew to my eyes, but they were not thetears of defeat; they were merely the involuntarytribute which nature paid to the departed tresses.

In a second my little jacket lay on the ground,and I stood on guard, resting lightly on my rightleg, and keeping my eye fixed steadily on Conway's^-in all of which I was faithfully following the in-structions of Phil Adams, whose father subscribedto a sporting journal.

Conway also threw himself into a defensive at-titude, and there we were, glaring at each other,motionless, neither of us disposed to risk an attack,but both on the alert to resist one. There is notelling how long we might have remained in thatabsurd position had we not been interrupted.

It was a custom with the larger pupils to returnto the playground after school, and play base-balluntil sundown. The town authorities had prohib-ited ball-playing on the Square, and, there beingno other available place, the boys fell back per-force on the school-yard. Just at this crisis adozen or so of the Templars entered the gate, and,seeing at a glance the belligerent status of Con-way and myself, dropped bat and ball and rushedto the spot where we stood.

" Is it a fight ? " asked Phil Adams, who saw byour freshness that we had not yet got to work.

" Yes, it 's a fight," I answered, " unless Con-way will ask Wallace's pardon, promise never tohector me in future — and put back my hair !"

This last condition was rather a staggerer.

"I shan't do nothing of the sort," said Con-way sulkily.

" Then the thing must go on," said Adams,with dignity. " Rodgers, as I understand it, isyour second, Conway ? Bailey, come here.What's the row about ? "

" He was thrashing Binny Wallace."

"No, I wasn't," interrupted Conway; "but I

was going to, because he knows who put Meeks'smortar over our door. And I know well enoughwho did it; it was that sneaking little mulatter !'— pointing at me.

" Oh, by George! " I cried, reddening at the in-sult.

" Cool is the word," said Adams, as he bound ahandkerchief round my head and carefully tuckedaway the long straggling locks that offered a

Preparing for tht Battle

tempting advantage to the enemy. "Who everheard of a fellow with such a head of hair goinginto action !' muttered Phil, twitching the hand-kerchief to ascertain if it were securely tied. Hethen loosened my gallowses (braces), and buckledthem tightly above my hips. " Now, then, ban-tam, never say die !'

Conway regarded these business-like prepara-

Ii6 THE STORY OF A BAD BOY

tions with evident misgiving, for he called Rod-gers to his side, and had himself arrayed in asimilar manner, though his hair was cropped soclose that you could not have taken hold of it witha pair of tweezers.

" Is your man ready?' asked Phil Adams, ad-i dressing Rodgers.

" Ready! "

" Keep your back to the gate, Tom," whisperedPhil in my ear, " and you '11 have the sun in hiseyes."

Behold us once more face to face, like Davidand the Philistine. Look at us as long as youmay; for this is all you shall see of the combat.According to my thinking, the hospital teaches abetter lesson than the battlefield. I will tell youabout my black eye, and my swollen lip, if youwill; but not a word of the fight.

You will get no description of it from me, sim-ply because I think it would prove very poor read-ing, and not because I consider my revolt againstConway's tyranny unjustifiable.

I had borne Conway's persecutions for manymonths with lamb-like patience. I might haveshielded myself by appealing to Mr. Grimshaw;but no boy in the Temple Grammar School coulddo that without losing caste. Whether this wasjust or not does not matter a pin, since it was so—•a traditionary law of the place. The personal in-convenience I suffered from my tormentor was

nothing to the pain he inflicted on me indirectlyby his persistent cruelty to little Binny Wallace.I should have lacked the spirit of a hen if I hadnot resented it finally. I am glad that I facedConway, and asked no favors, and got rid of himforever. I am glad that Phil Adams taught me tobox, and I say to all youngsters: Learn to box, toride, to pull an oar, and to swim. The occasionmay come round when a decent proficiency in oneor the rest of these accomplishments will be ofservice to you.

In one of the best booksI ever written for boysare these words : —

" Learn to box, then, as you learn to play cricketand foot-ball. Not one of you will be the worse,but very much the better, for learning to box well.Should you never have to use it in earnest, there 'sno exercise in the world so good for the temper,and for the muscles of the back and legs.

" As for fighting, keep out of it, if you can, byall means. When the time comes, if ever it should,that you have to say ' Yes' or ' No' to a challengeto fight, say * No ' if you can — only take care youmake it plain to yourself why you say ' No.' It'sa proof of the highest courage, if done from trueChristian motives. It's quite right and justifiableif done from a simple aversion to physical painand danger. But don't say ' No' because you feara licking and say or think it's because you fear

1 Tom Brown's School Days at Rugby.

THE STORY OF A BAD BOY

God, for that's neither Christian nor honest. Andif you do fight, fight it out; and don't give inwhile you can stand and see."

And don't give in while you can't! say I. ForI could stand very little, and see not at all (havingpummeled the school-pump for the last twenty1seconds), when Conway retired from the field. As^Phil Adams stepped up to shake hands with me,he received a telling blow in the stomach; for allthe fight was not out of me yet, and I mistook himfor a new adversary.

Convinced of my error, I accepted his congratu-lations, with those of the other boys, blandly andblindly. I remember that Binny Wallace wanted

to give me his silverpencil - case. Thegentle soul had stoodthroughout the con-test with his faceturned to the fence,suffering untold ag-ony.

A good wash at thepump, and a cold key *.applied to my eye, re-freshed me amazingly-Escorted by two or three of the schoolfellows, Iwalked home through the pleasant autumn twi-light, battered but triumphant. As I went along,my cap cocked on one side to keep the chilly air

Phil A dams shaking Hands

from my eye, I felt that I was not only following
my nose, but following it so closely, that I was in
some danger of treading on it.
I seemed to have nose enough
for the whole party. My left
cheek, also, was puffed out like
a dumpling. I could not help
saying to myself, " If this is
victory, how about that other
fellow ?"

" Tom," said Harry Blake,hesitating.
Afterwards
" Well ?"

" Did you see Mr. Grimshaw looking out of therecitation-room window just as we left the yard?"

" No ; was he, though ?"

" I am sure of it."

" Then he must have seen all the row."

" Should n't wonder."

" No, he did n't," broke in Adams, " or he wouldhave stopped it short metre; but I guess he sawyou pitching into the pump — which you did un-commonly strong — and of course he smelt mis-chief directly.'

" Well, it can't be helped now," I reflected.

" — As the monkey said when he fell out of thecocoanut tree," added Charley Marden, trying tomake me laugh.

It was early candle-light when we reached thehouse. Miss Abigail, opening the front door,
started back at my hilarious appearance. I triedto smile upon her sweetly, but the smile ripplingover my swollen cheek, and dying away like aspent wave on my nose, produced an expression ofwhich Miss Abigail declared she had never seenthe like excepting on the face of a

Chinese idol.j She hustled me unceremoniously into the pres-ence of my grandfather in the sitting-room. Cap-tain Nutter, as the recognized professional warriorof our family, could not consistently take me totask for fighting Conway ; nor was he disposed todo so; for the Captain was well aware of the long-continued provocation I had endured.

" Ah, you rascal ! " cried the old gentleman, af-ter hearing my story, "just like me when I wasyoung — always in one kind of trouble or another.I believe it runs in the family."

" I think," said Miss Abigail, without the faint-est expression on her countenance, " that a table-spoonful of hot-dro— "

The Captain interrupted Miss Abigail peremp-torily, directing her to make a shade out of card-board and black silk, to tie over my eye. MissAbigail must have been possessed with the ideathat I had taken up pugilism as a profession, forshe turned out no fewer than six of these blinders.

" They be handy to have in the house," saidMiss Abigail grimly.

Of course, so great a breach of discipline wasnot to be passed over by Mr. Grimshaw. He had,

as we suspected, witnessed the closing scene of thefight from the schoolroom window, and the nextmorning, after prayers, I was not wholly unpre-pared when Master Conway and myself were calledup to the desk for examination. Conway, with apiece of court-plaster in the shape of a Maltesecross on his right cheek, and I with the silk patchover my left eye, caused a general titter throughthe room.

" Silence ! " said Mr. Grimshaw sharply.

As the reader is already familiar with the lead-ing points in the case of Bailey versus Conway, Ishall not report the trial further than to say thatAdams, Marden, and several other pupils testifiedto the fact that Conway had imposed on me eversince my first day at the Temple School. Theirevidence also went to show that Conway was aquarrelsome character generally. Bad for Conway.Seth Rodgers, on the part of his friend, provedthat I had struck the first blow. That was bad forme.

" If you please, sir," said Binny Wallace, hold-ing up his hand for permission to speak, " Baileydid n't fight on his own account; he fought on myi.account, and, if you please, sir, I am the boy to beblamed, for I was the cause of the trouble."

This drew out the story of Conway's harsh treat-]ment of the smaller boys. As Binny related thewrongs of his playfellows, saying very little of hisown grievances, I noticed that Mr. Grimshaw's

hand, unknown to himself perhaps, rested lightlyfrom time to time on Wallace's sunny hair. Theexamination finished, Mr. Grimshaw leaned on thedesk thoughtfully for a moment, and then said : —

" Every boy in this school knows that it isagainst the rules to fight. If one boy maltreatsanother, within school-bounds, or within school-hours, that is a matter for me to settle. The caseshould be laid before me. I disapprove of tale-bearing, I never encourage it in the slightest de-gree ; but when one pupil systematically persecutesa schoolmate, it is the duty of some head-boy toinform me. No pupil has a right to take the lawinto his own hands. If there is any fighting to bedone, I am the person to be consulted. I disap-prove of boys' fighting; it is unnecessary and un-christian. In the present instance, I considerevery large boy in this school at fault; but as theoffense is one of omission rather than commission,my punishment must rest only on the two boysconvicted of misdemeanor. Conway loses his re-cess for a month, and Bailey has a page added tohis Latin lessons for the next four recitations. Inow request Bailey and Conway to shake hands inthe presence of the school, and acknowledge theirregret at what has occurred."

Conway and I approached each other slowly andcautiously, as if we were bent upon another hostilecollision. We clasped hands in the tamest man-ner imaginable, and Conway mumbled, " I 'm sorryI fought with you."

"I think you are," I replied, drily, "and I'msorry I had to thrash you."

" You can go to your seats," said Mr. Grimshaw,turning his face aside to hide a smile. I am suremy apology was a very good one.

I never had any more trouble with Conway.He and his shadow, Seth Rodgers, gave me a wideberth for many months. Nor was Binny Wallacesubjected to further molestation. Miss Abigail'ssanitary stores, including a bottle of opodeldoc,were never called into requisition. The six blacksilk patches, with their elastic strings, are stilldangling from a beam in the garret of the NutterHouse, waiting for me to get into fresh difficulties.

CHAPTER XI

ALL ABOUT GYPSY

THIS record of my life at Rivermouth would bestrangely incomplete did I not devote an entirechapter to Gypsy. I had other pets, of course;for what healthy boy could long exist without nu-merous friends in the animal kingdom ? I had twowhite mice that were forever gnawing their wayout of a pasteboard chateau, and crawling over myface when I lay asleep. I used to keep the pink-eyed little beggars in my bedroom, greatly to theannoyance of Miss Abigail, who was constantlyfancying that one of the mice had secreted itselfsomewhere about her person.

I also owned a dog, a terrier, who managed insome inscrutable way to pick a quarrel with themoon, and on bright nights kept up such a ki-yi-ing in our back garden that we were finally forcedto dispose of him at private sale. He was purchasedby Mr. Oxford, the butcher. I protested againstthe arrangement, and ever afterwards, when wehad sausages from Mr. Oxford's shop, I made be-lieve I detected in them certain evidences thatCato had been foully dealt with.

Of birds I had no end — robins, purple-martins,

wrens, bulfinches, bobolinks, ringdoves, and pi-geons. At one time I took solid comfort in theiniquitous society of a dissipated old parrot, whotalked so terribly that the Rev. Wibird Hawkins,happening toget a sample ofPoll's vitupera-tive powers, pro-nounced him "abenighted hea-then," and ad-vised the Cap-tain to get rid ofhim. A braceof turtles sup-planted the par-rot in my affec-tions; the turtlesgave way to rab-bits ; and the rabbits in turn yielded to the superiorcharms of a small monkey, which the Captainbought of a sailor lately from the coast of Africa.

But Gypsy was the prime favorite, in spite ofmany rivals. I never grew weary of her. Shewas the most knowing little thing in the world.Her proper sphere in life — and the one to whichshe ultimately attained — was the saw-dust arenaof a traveling circus. There was nothing short ofthe three R's, reading, 'riting, and 'rithmetic, thatGypsy could not be taught. The gift of speechwas not hers, but the faculty of thought was.

Rev. Wibird Hawkins and Poll

My little friend, to be sure, was not exempt from certain graceful weaknesses, inseparable, perhaps, from the female character. She was very pretty, and she knew it. She was also passionately fond of dress — by which I mean her best harness. When she had this on, her curvetings and prancings were laughable, though in ordinary tackle she went along demurely enough. There was something in the enameled leather and the silver-washed mount-ings that chimed with her artistic sense. To have her mane braided, and a rose or a pansy stuck into her forelock, was to make her too conceited for anything.

She had another trait not rare among her sex. She liked the attentions of young gentlemen, while the society of girls bored her. She would drag them, sulkily, in the cart; but as for permitting one of them in the saddle, the idea was preposter-ous. Once when Pepper Whitcomb's sister, inspite of our remonstrances, ventured to mount her, Gypsy gave a little indignant neigh, and tossed the gentle Emma heels over head in no time. But with any of the boys the mare was as docile as a lamb.

Her treatment of the several members of the family was comical. For the Captain she enter-tained a wholesome respect, and was always on her good behavior when he was around. As to Miss Abigail, Gypsy simply laughed at her — literally laughed, contracting her upper lip and displaying

127

all her snow-white teeth, as if something about Miss Abigail struck her, Gypsy, as being extremely ridiculous.

Kitty Collins, for some reason or another, was afraid of the pony, or pretended to be. The saga-cious little animal knew it, of course, and fre-quently, when Kitty was hanging out clothes near the stable, the mare, being loose in the yard, would make short plunges at her. Once Gypsy seized the basket of clothespins with her teeth, and rising on her hind legs, pawing the air with her forefeet, followed Kitty clear up to the scullery steps.

That part of the yard was shut off from the rest by a gate; but no gate was proof against Gypsy's ingenuity. She could let down bars, lift up latches, draw bolts, and turn all sorts of buttons. This accomplishment rendered it hazardous for Miss Abigail or Kitty to leave any

Gypsy's Lunch

eatables on the kitchen table near the window. On one occasion Gypsy put in her head and lapped up six custard pies that had been placed by the casement to cool.

An account of my young lady's various pranks would fill a thick volume. A favorite trick of hers, on being requested to "walk like Miss Abi-gail," was to assume a little skittish gait so true to nature that Miss Abigail herself was obliged to admit the cleverness of the imitation.

The idea of putting Gypsy through a system-atic course of instruction was suggested to me by a visit to the circus which gave an annual per-formance in Rivermouth. This show embraced among its attractions a number of trained Shet-land ponies, and I determined that Gypsy should likewise have the benefit of a liberal education. I succeeded in teaching her to waltz, to fire a pistol by tugging at a string tied to the trigger, to lie down dead, to wink one eye, and to execute many other feats of a difficult nature. She took to her studies admirably, and enjoyed the whole thing as much as any one.

The monkey was a perpetual marvel to Gypsy. They became bosom-friends in an incredibly brief period, and were never easy out of each other's sight. Prince Zany — that 's what Pepper Whit-comb and I christened him one day, much to the disgust of the monkey, who bit a piece out of Pep-per's nose — resided in the stable, and went to roost every night on the pony's back, where I usu?

ally found him in the morning. Whenever I rode out I was obliged to secure his Highness the Prince with a stout cord to the fence, he chatter-ing all the time like a madman.

One afternoon as I was cantering through the crowded part of the town, I noticed that the peo-ple in the street stopped, stared at me, and fell to laughing. I turned round in the saddle, and there was Zany, with a great burdock leaf in his paw, perched up behind me on the crupper, as solemn as a judge.

After a few months, poor Zany sickened myste-riously and died. The dark thought occurred to me then, and comes back to me now with re-doubled force, that Miss Abigail must have given him some hot-drops. Zany left a large circle of sorrowing friends, if not relatives. Gypsy, I think, never entirely recovered from the shock occasioned by his early demise. She became fonder of me, though; and one of her cunningest demonstra-tions was to escape from the stable-yard, and trot up to the door of the Temple Grammar School, where I would discover her at recess patientlywaiting for me, with her forefeet on the secondstep, and wisps of straw standing out all over her,like quills upon the fretful porcupine.

I should fail if I tried to tell you how dear thepony was to me. Even hard, unloving men be-come attached to the horses they take care of; soI, who was neither unloving nor hard, grew to loveevery glossy hair of the pretty little creature that

depended on me for her soft straw bed and herdaily modicum of oats. In my prayer at night Inever forgot to mention Gypsy with the rest ofthe family — generally setting forthher claims first.

Whatever relates to Gypsy belongsproperly to this narrative ; thereforeI offer no apology for rescuing fromoblivion, and boldly printing here ashort composition which I wrote inthe early part of my first quarter atthe Temple Grammar School. It ismy maiden effort in a difficult art, andis, perhaps, lacking in those graces ofthought and style which are reachedonly after the severest practice.

Every Wednesday morning on en-tering school, each pupil was expectedto lay his exercise on Mr. Grimshaw'sdesk; the subject was usually selectedby Mr. Grimshaw himself, the Monday previous.With a humor characteristic of him, our teacherhad instituted two prizes, one for the best and theother for the worst composition of the month.The first prize consisted of a penknife, or a pencil-case, or some such article dear to the heart ofyouth ; the second prize entitled the winner towear for an hour or two a sort of conical papercap, on the front of which was written, in tallletters, this modest admission: I AM A DUNCE!

Prize No. a

The competitor who took prize No. 2 was not gen-erally an object of envy.

My pulse beat high with pride and expectationthat Wednesday morning, as I laid my essay, neatlyfolded, on the master's table. I firmly decline tosay which prize I won ; but here is the composi-tion to speak for itself : —

It is no small-author vanity that induces me topublish this stray leaf of natural history. I lay itbefore our young folks, not for their admiration,but for their criticism. Let each reader take hislead pencil and remorselessly correct the ortho-graphy, the capitalization, and the punctuation ofthe essay. I shall not feel hurt at seeing mytreatise cut all to pieces; though I think highlyof the production, not on account of its literaryexcellence, which I candidly admit is not overpow-ering, but because it was written years and yearsago about Gypsy, by a little fellow who, when Istrive to recall him, appears to me like a reducedghost of my present self.

I am confident that any reader who has ever hadpets, birds or animals, will forgive me for this briefdigression.

CHAPTER XII

WINTER AT RIVERMOUTH

" I GUESS we 're going to have a regular old-fashioned snowstorm," said Captain Nutter, onebleak December morning, casting a peculiarlynautical glance skyward.

The Captain was always hazarding propheciesabout the weather, which somehow never turnedout according to his prediction. The vanes onthe church steeples seemed to take a cynicalpleasure in humiliating the dear old gentleman.If he said it was going to be a clear day, a densesea fog was pretty certain to set in before noon.Once he caused a protracted drought by assuringus every morning, for six consecutive weeks, thatit would rain in a few hours. But, sure enough,that afternoon it began snowing.

Now I had not seen a snowstorm since I waseighteen months old, and of course rememberednothing about it. A boy familiar from his infancywith the rigors of our New England winters canform no idea of the impression made on me bythis natural phenomenon. My delight and sur-prise were as boundless as if the heavy gray skyhad let down a shower of pond-lilies and white

roses, instead of snowflakes. It happened to bea half-holiday, so I had nothing to do but watchthe feathery crystals whirling hither and thitherthrough the air. I stood by the sitting-room win-dow gazing at the wonder until twilight shut outthe novel scene.

We had had several slight flurries of hail andsnow before, but this was a regular nor'easter.

Several inches of snow had already fallen. Therosebushes at the door drooped with the weight oftheir magical blossoms, and the two posts thatheld the garden gate were transformed into statelyTurks, with white turbans, guarding the entranceto the Nutter House.

The storm increased at sundown, and continuedwith unabated violence through the night. Thenext morning, when I jumped out of bed, the sunwas shining brightly, the cloudless heavens worethe tender azure of June, and the whole earth laymuffled up to the eyes, as it were, in a thick man-tle of milk-white down.

It was a very deep snow. The Oldest Inhabit-ant (what would become of a New England townor village without its oldest inhabitant?) overhauledhis almanacs, and pronounced it the deepest snowwe had had for twenty years. It could n't havebeen much deeper without smothering us all. Ourstreet was a sight to be seen, or, rather, it was asight not to be seen ; for very little street wasvisible. One huge drift completely banked up

'35

our front door and half covered my bedroom win-dow.

There was no school that day, for all the thor-oughfares were impassable. By twelve o'clock,however, the great snow-ploughs, each drawn byfour yokes of oxen, broke a wagon-path throughthe principal streets ; but the foot-passengers hada hard time of it floundering in the arctic drifts.

The Captain and I cut a tunnel, three feet wideand six feet high, from our front door to the side-walk opposite. It was a beautiful cavern, with itswalls and roof inlaid with mother-of-pearl and dia-

Talking over the Great Storm

monds. I am sure the ice palace of the RussianEmpress, in Cowper's poem, was not a more su-perb piece of architecture.

The thermometer began falling shortly beforesunset, and we had the bitterest cold night I everexperienced. This brought out the Oldest Inhab-itant again the next day — and what a gay

old boy

he was for deciding everything! Our tunnel wasturned into solid ice. A crust thick enough tobear men and horses had formed over the snoweverywhere, and the air was alive with merry sleigh-bells. Icy stalactites, a yard long, hung from theeaves of the house, and the Turkish sentinels atthe gate looked as if they had given up all hopesof ever being relieved from duty.

So the winter set in cold and glittering. Every-thing out of doors was sheathed in silver mail. Toquote from Charley Marden, it was " cold enoughto freeze the tail off a brass monkey " — an ob-servation which seemed to me extremely happy,though I knew little or nothing concerning theendurance of brass monkeys, having never seenone.

I had looked forward to the advent of the seasonwith grave apprehensions, nerving myself to meetdreary nights and monotonous days ; but summeritself was not more jolly than winter at Rivermouth.Snow-balling at school, skating on the Mill Pond,coasting by moonlight, long rides behind Gypsy ina brand-new little sleigh built expressly for her,were sports no less exhilarating than those whichbelonged to the sunny months. And then Thanks-giving! The nose of Memory — why should notMemory have a nose ? — dilates with pleasure overthe rich perfume of Miss Abigail's forty mince-pies, each one more delightful than the other, likethe Sultan's forty wives. Christmas was another

red-letter day, though it was not so generally ob-served in New England as it is now.

The great wood-fire in the tiled chimney-placemade our sitting-room very cheerful of winternights. When the north-wind howled about theeaves, and the sharp fingers of the sleet tappedagainst the window-panes, it was nice to be sowarmly sheltered fromthe storm. A dish ofapples and a pitcherof chilly cider werealways served duringthe evening. TheCaptain had a funnyway of leaning backin the chair and eat-ing his apple with hiseyes closed. Some-times I played domi-noes with him, andsometimes Miss Abigail read aloud to us, pronoun-cing "to" toe, and sounding all the eds.

In a former chapter I alluded to Miss Abigail'smanaging propensities. She had effected manychanges in the Nutter House before I came thereto live; but there was one thing against whichshe had long contended without being able to over-come. This was the Captain's pipe. On firsttaking command of the household, she prohibitedsmoking in the sitting-room, where it had been the

Eating his Apple

old gentleman's custom to take a whiff or two ofthe fragrant weed after meals. The edict wentforth —and so did the pipe. An excellent move,no doubt; but then the house was his, and if hesaw fit to keep a tub of tobacco burning in themiddle of the parlor floor, he had a perfect rightto do so. However, he humored her in this as inother matters, and smoked by stealth, like a guiltycreature, in the barn, or about the gardens. Thatwas practicable in summer, but in winter the

Cap-tain was hard put to it. When he could not standit longer, he retreated to his bedroom and barri-caded the door. Such was the position of affairsat the time of which I write.

One morning, a few days after the great snow,as Miss Abigail was dusting the chronometer inthe hall, she beheld Captain Nutter slowly descend-ing the staircase, with a long clay pipe in hismouth. Miss Abigail could hardly credit her owneyes.

" Dan'el!' she gasped, retiring heavily on thehat-rack.

The tone of reproach with which this word wasuttered failed to produce the slightest effect onthe Captain, who merely removed the pipe fromhis lips for an instant, and blew a cloud into thechilly air. The thermometer stood at two degreesbelow zero in our hall.

"Dan'el!" cried Miss Abigail, hysterically —"Dan'el, don't come near me !" Whereupon she

fainted away ; for the smell of tobacco smoke al-ways made her deadly sick.

Kitty Collins rushed from the kitchen with abasin of water, and set to work bathing Miss Abi-gail's temples and chafing her hands. I thoughtmy grandfather rather cruel, as he stood there

Kitty and Tom enjoying the Joke

with a half-smile on his countenance, complacentlywatching Miss Abigail's sufferings. When shewas "brought to," the Captain sat down besideher, and, with a lovely twinkle in his eye, saidsoftly:

" Abigail, my dear, there was n't any tobacco inthat pipe ! It was a new pipe. I fetched it downfor Tom to blow soap-bubbles with."

At these words Kitty Collins hurried away, herfeatures working strangely. Several minutes laterI came upon her in the scullery with the greaterportion of a crash towel stuffed into her mouth."Miss Abygil smelt the terbacca with her oi!"cried Kitty, partially removing the cloth, and thenimmediately stopping herself up again.

The Captain's joke furnished us — that is, Kittyand me — with mirth for many a day; as to MissAbigail, I think she never wholly pardoned him.After this, Captain Nutter gradually gave upsmoking, which is an untidy, injurious, disgrace-ful, and highly pleasant habit.

A boy's life in a secluded New England townin winter does not afford many points for illus-tration. Of course he gets his ears or toes frost-bitten ; of course he smashes his sled againstanother boy's; of course he bangs his head on theice, and he 's a lad of no enterprise whatever ifhe does not manage to skate into an eel-hole, andbe brought home half-drowned. All these thingshappened to me; but, as they lack novelty, I passthem over to tell you about the famous snow-fortwhich we built on Slatter's Hill.

CHAPTER XIII

THE SNOW-FORT ON SLATTER *S HILL

THE memory of man, even that of the OldestInhabitant, runneth not back to the time whenthere did not exist a feud between the NorthEnd and the South End boys of Rivermouth.

The origin of the feud is involved in mystery;it is impossible to say which party was the firstaggressor in the far-off ante-revolutionary ages ;but the fact remains that the youngsters of thoseantipodal sections entertained a mortal hatred foreach other, and that this hatred had been handeddown from generation to generation, like MilesStandish's punch-bowl.

I know not what laws, natural or unnatural,regulated the warmth of the quarrel; but at someseasons it raged more violently than at others.This winter both parties were unusually lively andantagonistic. Great was the wrath of the South-Enders when they discovered that the North-Enders had thrown up a fort on the crown ofSlatter's Hill.

Slatter's Hill, or No-man's-land, as it was gener-ally called, was a rise of ground covering, perhaps,an acre and a quarter, situated on an imaginary

line, marking the boundary between the two dis*tricts. An immense stratum of granite, whichhere and there thrust out a wrinkled bowlder, pre-, vented the site from being used for building pur-poses. The street ran on either side of the hill,from one part of which a quantity of rock hadbeen removed to form the underpinning of thenew jail. This excavation made the approach fromthat point all but impossible, especially when theragged ledges were a-glitter with ice. You seewhat a spot it was for a snow-fort.

One evening twenty or thirty of the North-Enders quietly took possession of Slatter's Hill,and threw up a strong line of breastworks, some-thing after this shape:

The rear of the intrenchment, being protectedby the quarry, was left open. The walls were fourfeet high, and twenty-two inches thick, strength-ened at the angles by stakes driven firmly into theground.

Fancy the rage of the South-Enders the nextday, when they spied our snowy citadel, with Jack

Harris's red silk pocket-handkerchief floating de-fiantly from the flagstaff.

In less than an hour it was known all overtown, in military circles at least, that the " Puddle-dockers " and the " River-rats " (these were thederisive sub-titles bestowed on our South-Endfoes) intended to attack the fort that Saturdayafternoon.

At two o'clock all the fighting boys of theTemple Grammar School, and as many recruitsas we could muster, lay behind the walls of FortSlatter, with three hundred compact snow-ballspiled up in pyramids, awaiting the approach ofthe enemy. The enemy was not slow in makinghis approach — fifty strong, headed by one MatAmes. Our forces were under the command ofGeneral J. Harris.

Before the action commenced, a meeting wasarranged between the rival commanders, whodrew up and signed certain rules and regulationsrespecting the conduct of the battle. As it wasimpossible for the North-Enders to occupy the fortpermanently, it was stipulated that the South-Enders should assault it only on Wednesday andSaturday afternoons between the hours of two andsix. For them to take possession of the place atany other time was not to constitute a capture, but,on the contrary, was to be considered a dishonora-ble and cowardly act.

THE STORY OF A BAD BOY

The North-Enders, on the other hand, agreed togive up the fort whenever ten of the storming party succeeded in obtaining at one time a footing on the parapet, and were able to hold the same for the space of two minutes. Both sides were to abstain from putting pebbles into their snow-balls,, nor was it permissible to use frozen ammunition, j

A snow - ball soaked in water and left out to cool was a pro-jectile which in previous years had been re-sorted to with disastrous re-sults.

These prelim-inaries settled, the command-ers retired to their respective corps. The interview had taken place on the hill-side between the opposing lines.

General Harris divided his men into two bodies ; the first comprised the most skillful marksmen, or gunners ; the second, the reserve force, was com-posed of the strongest boys, whose duty it was to repel the scaling parties, and to make occasional

The Commanders

sallies for the purpose of capturing prisoners, who were bound by the articles of treaty to faithfully serve under our flag until they were exchanged at the close of the day.

The repellers were called light infantry; but when they carried on operations beyond the fort they became cavalry. It was also their duty, when not otherwise engaged, to manufacture snow-balls. The General's staff consisted of five Templars (I among the number, with the rank of Major), who carried the General's orders and looked after the wounded.

General Mat Ames, a veteran commander, was no less wide-awake in the disposition of his army. Five companies, each numbering but six men, in order not to present too big a target to our sharp-shooters, were to charge the fort from different points, their advance being covered by a heavy fire from the gunners posted in the rear. Each sealer was provided with only two rounds of ammunition, which were not to be used until he had mounted the breastwork and could deliver his shots on our heads.

The following diagram represents the interior of the fort just previous to the assault. Nothing on earth could represent the state of things after the first volley.

THE STORY OF A BAD BOY

a. Flagstaff. C. Ammunition. ",! Gunners in position.

b. General Harris and his Staff, d. Hospital. g,g. The quarry.

e, e. Reserve corps.

The enemy was posted thus :

a, a. The five attacking columns, b, . Artillery, c. General Ames's head-quarters.

The thrilling moment had now arrived. If I had been going into a real engagement I could not have been more deeply impressed by the impor-tance of the occasion.

The fort opened fire first — a single ball from the dexterous hand of General Harris taking

Gen-eral Ames in the very pit of his stomach. Acheer went up from Fort Slatter. In an instantthe air was thick with flying missiles, in the midstof which we dimly descried the storming partiessweeping up the hill, shoulder to shoulder. The

shouts of the leaders, and the snow-balls burstinglike shells about our ears, made it very lively.

Not more than a dozen of the enemy succeededin reaching the crest of the hill; five of theseclambered upon the icy walls, where they wereinstantly grabbed by the legs and jerked into thefort. The rest retired confused and blinded byour well-directed fire.

When General Harris (with his right eye bungedup) said, " Soldiers, I am proud of you !" my heartswelled in my bosom.

The victory, however, had not been without itsprice. Six North-Enders, having rushed out toharass the discomfited enemy, were gallantly cutoff by General Ames and captured. Among thesewere Lieutenant P. Whitcomb (who had no busi-ness to join in the charge, being weak in the knees)and Captain Fred Langdon, of General Harris'sstaff. Whitcomb was one of the most notableshots on our side, though he was not much toboast of in a rough-and-tumble fight, owing to theweakness before mentioned. General Ames puthim among the gunners, and we were quickly madeaware of the loss we had sustained, by receivinga frequent artful ball which seemed to light withunerring instinct on any nose that was the leastbit exposed. I have known one of Pepper's snow-balls, fired point-blank, to turn a corner and hit aboy who considered himself absolutely safe.

But we had no time for vain regrets. The bat-

tie raged. Already there were two bad cases ofblack-eye, and one of nose-bleed, in the hospital.

It was glorious excitement, those pell-mell on-slaughts and hand-to-hand struggles. Twice wewere within an ace of being driven from ourstronghold, when General Harris and his staff1 leaped recklessly upon the ramparts and hurledthe besiegers heels over head downhill.

At sunset the garrison of Fort Slatter was stillunconquered, and the South - Enders, in a solidphalanx, marched off whistling " Yankee Doodle,"while we cheered and jeered them until they wereout of hearing.

General Ames remained behind to effect an ex-change of prisoners. We held thirteen of his men,and he eleven of ours. General Ames proposed tocall it an even thing, since many of his eleven pris-oners were officers, while nearly all our thirteencaptives were privates. A dispute arising on thispoint, the two noble generals came to fisticuffs,and in the fracas our brave commander got hisremaining well eye badly damaged. This did notprevent him from writing a general order the nextday, on a slate, in which he complimented thetroops on their heroic behavior.

On the following Wednesday the siege was re-newed I forget whether it was on that afternoonor the next that we lost Fort Slatter; but lose itwe did, with much valuable ammunition and sev-eral men. After a series of desperate assaults,

we forced General Ames to capitulate; and he, inturn, made the place too hot to hold us. So fromday to day the tide of battle surged to and fro,sometimes favoring our arms, and sometimes thoseof the enemy.

General Ames handled his men with great skill;his deadliest foe could not deny that. Once heout-generaled our commander in the followingmanner : He massed his gunners on our left andopened a brisk fire, under cover of which a singlecompany (six men) advanced on that angle of thefort. Our reserves on the right rushed over todefend the threatened point. Meanwhile, fourcompanies of the enemy's sealers made a detourround the foot of the hill, and dashed into FortSlatter without opposition. At the same momentGeneral Ames's gunners closed in on our left, andthere we were between two fires. Of course wehad to vacate the fort. A cloud rested on GeneralHarris's military reputation until his superior tac-tics enabled him to dispossess the enemy.

As the winter wore on, the war-spirit waxedfiercer and fiercer. Finally the provision againstusing heavy substances in the snow-balls was dis-regarded. A ball stuck full of sand-bird shotcame tearing into Fort Slatter. In retaliation,General Harris ordered a broadside of shells ; i.

e.snow-balls containing marbles. After this, bothsides never failed to freeze their ammunition.

It was no longer child's play to march up to the

walls of Fort Slatter, nor was the position of thebesieged less perilous. At every assault three orfour boys on each side were disabled. It was notan infrequent occurrence for the combatants tohold up a flag of truce while they removed someinsensible comrade.

Matters grew worse and worse. Seven North-Enders had been seriously wounded, and a dozenSouth-Enders were reported on the sick list. Theselectmen of the town awoke to the fact of whatwas going on, and detailed a posse of police toprevent further disturbance. The boys at the footof the hill, South-Enders as it happened, findingthemselves assailed in the rear and on the flank,turned round and attempted to beat off the watch-men. In this they were sustained by numerousvolunteers from the fort, who looked upon theinterference as tyrannical.

The watch were determined fellows, and chargedthe boys valiantly, driving them all into the fort,where we made common cause, fighting side byside like the best of friends. In vain the fourguardians of the peace rushed up the hill, flourish-ing their clubs and calling upon us to surrender.They could not get within ten yards of the fort,our fire was so destructive. In one of the onsetsa man named Mugridge, more valorous than hispeers, threw himself upon the parapet, when hewas seized by twenty pairs of hands, and draggedinside the breastwork, where fifteen boys sat downon him to keep fyini quiet.

THE SNOW-FORT ON SLATTER'S HILL 153

Perceiving that it was impossible with theirsmall number to dislodge us, the watch sent forreinforcements. Their call was responded to,not only by the whole constabulary force (eightmen), but by a numerous body of citizens, who

The Unsuccessful Attack

had become alarmed at the prospect of a riot.This formidable array brought us to our senses:we began to think that maybe discretion was thebetter part of valor. General Harris and GeneralAmes, with their respective staffs, held a councilof war in the hospital, and a backward move-ment was decided on. So, after one grand fare-well volley, we fled, sliding, jumping, rolling,

tumbling down the quarry at the rear of the fort,and escaped without losing a man.

But we lost Fort Slatter forever. Those battle-scarred ramparts were razed to the ground, andhumiliating ashes sprinkled over the historic spot,near which a solitary lynx-eyed policeman wasseen prowling from time to time during the restof the winter.

The event passed into a legend, and afterwards,when later instances of pluck and endurancewere spoken of, the boys would say, " By golly!you ought to have been at the fights on Slatter'sHill 1"

CHAPTER XIV

THE CRUISE OF THE DOLPHIN

IT was spring again. The snow had fadedaway like a dream, and we were awakened, so tospeak, by the sudden chirping of robins in ourback garden. Marvelous transformation of snow-drifts into lilacs, wondrous miracle of the unfold-ing leaf! We read in the Holy Book how ourSaviour, at the marriage-feast, changed the waterinto wine; we pause and wonder, but every houra greater miracle is wrought at our feet, if we havebut eyes to see it.

I had now been a year at Rivermouth. If youdo not know what sort of boy I was, it is not be-cause I have been lacking in frankness with you.Of my progress at school I say little; for this isa story, pure and simple, and not a treatise on edu-cation. Behold me, however, well up in most ofthe classes. I have worn my Latin grammar into:tatters, and am in the first book of Virgil. I in-!terlard my conversation at home with easy quo- jtations from that poet, and impress Captain jNutter with a lofty notion of my learning. I amlikewise translating Les Aventures de Telemaquefrom the French, and shall tackle Blair's Lectures

156 THE STORY OF A BAD BOY

the next term. I am ashamed of my crude com-position about The Horse, and can do better now.Sometimes my head almost aches with the varietyof my knowledge. I consider Mr. Grimshaw thegreatest scholar that ever lived, and I do not knowwhich I would rather be — a learned man likehim, or a circus-rider.

My thoughts revert to this particular springmore frequently than to any other period of myboyhood, for it was marked by an event that leftan indelible impression on my memory. As Ipen these pages, I feel that I am writing ofsomething which happened yesterday, so vividlyit all comes back to me.

Every Rivermouth boy looks upon the sea asbeing in some way mixed up with his destiny.While he is yet a baby lying in his cradle, he hearsthe dull, far-off boom of the breakers; when he isolder, he wanders by the sandy shore, watchingthe waves that come plunging up the beach likewhite-maned sea-horses, as Thoreau calls them ;his eye follows the lessening sail as it fades intothe blue horizon, and he burns for the time whenhe shall stand on the quarter-deck of his own ship,and go sailing proudly across that mysteriouswaste of waters.

Then the town itself is full of hints and flavorsof the sea. The gables and roofs of the housesfacing eastward are covered with red rust, like theflukes of old anchors; a salty smell pervades the

air, and dense gray fogs, the very breath of Ocean,periodically creep up into the quiet streets andenvelop everything. The terrific storms thatlash the coast; the kelp and spars, and sometimesthe bodies of drowned men, tossed on shore by thescornful waves; the shipyards, the wharves, andthe tawny fleet of fishing-smacks yearly fitted outat Rivermouth — these things, and a hundredother, feed the imagination and fill the brain ofevery healthy boy with dreams of adventure. Helearns to swim almost as soon as he can walk; hedraws in with his mother's milk the art of hand-ling an oar: he is born a sailor, whatever he mayturn out to be afterwards.

To own the whole or a portion of a row-boat ishis earliest ambition. No wonder that I, born tothis life, and coming back to it with freshest sym-pathies, should have caught the prevailing in-fection. No wonder I longed to buy a part of thetrim little sail-boat Dolphin, which chanced justthen to be in the market. This was in the latterpart of May.

Three shares, at five or six dollars each, I for-get which, had already been taken by Phil Adams, Fred Langdon, and Binny Wallace. The fourth and remaining share hung fire. Unless a pur-chaser could be found for this, the bargain was to fall through.

I am afraid I required but slight urging to join in the investment I had four dollars and fifty

cents on hand, and the treasur-er of the Centi-pedes advanced me the balance, receiving my silver pencil-case as ample security. It was a proud moment when I stood on the wharf with my partners, in-specting the Dolphin, moored at the foot of a very slippery flight of steps. She was painted white with a green stripe out-side, and on the stern a yellow dolphin, with its scarlet mouth wide open, stared with a surprised expression at its own reflection in the water. The boat was a great bargain.

I whirled my cap in the air, and ran to the stairs leading down from the wharf, when a hand was laid gently on my shoulder. I turned, and faced Captain Nutter. I never saw such an old sharp-eye as he was in those days.

I faced Captain Nutter

I knew he would not be angry with me for buying a row-boat; but I also knew that the little bowsprit suggesting a jib, and the tapering mast ready for its few square feet of canvas, were trifles not likely to meet his approval. As far as rowing on the river, among the wharves, was concerned, the Captain had long since withdrawn his decided objections, having convinced himself, by going out with me several times, that I could manage a pair of sculls as well as anybody.

I was right in my surmises. He commanded me, in the most emphatic terms, never to go out in the Dolphin without leaving the mast in the boat-house. This curtailed my anticipated sport, but the pleasure of having a pull whenever I wanted it remained. I never disobeyed the Captain's orders touching the sail, though I sometimes ex-tended my row beyond the points he had indi-cated.

The river was dangerous for sail-boats. Squalls, without the slightest warning, were of frequent occurrence; scarcely a year passed that three or four persons were not drowned under the very windows of the town, and these, oddly enough, were generally sea-captains, who either did not understand the river, or lacked the skill to handle a small craft.

A knowledge of such disasters, one of which I witnessed, consoled me somewhat when I saw Phil Adams skimming over the water in a spanking

breeze with every stitch of canvas set. There were few better yachtsmen than Phil Adams. He usually went sailing alone, for both Langdon and Binny Wallace were under the same restrictions I was.

Not long after the purchase of the boat, we planned an excursion to Sandpeep Island, the last of the islands in the harbor. We purposed to start early in the morning, and return with the tide in the moonlight. Our only difficulty was to obtain a whole day's exemption from school, the customary half-holiday not being long enough for our picnic. Somehow, we could not work it; but fortune arranged it for us. I may say here, that, whatever else I did, I never played truant(" hookey " we called it) in my life.

One afternoon the four owners of the Dolphin exchanged significant glances when Mr. Grimshaw announced from the desk that there would be no school the following day, he having just received intelligence of the death of his uncle in Boston. I was sincerely attached to Mr. Grimshaw, but I am afraid that the death of his uncle did not affect me as it ought to have done.

We were up before sunrise the next morning, in order to take advantage of the flood tide, which waits for no man. Our preparations for the cruise were made the previous evening. In the way of eatables and drinkables, we had stored in the stern of the Dolphin a generous bag of hard-tack

(for the chowder), a piece of pork to fry the cun-ners in, three gigantic apple-pies (bought at Pet-tingil's), half a dozen lemons, and a keg of springwater — the last-named article we slung over the side, to keep it cool, as soon as we got under way. The crockery and the bricks for our camp-stove we placed in the bows with the groceries, which included sugar, pepper, salt, and a bottle of pickles, Phil Adams contributed to the outfit a small tent of unbleached cotton cloth, under which we in-tended to take our nooning.

We unshipped the mast, threw in an extra oar, and were ready to embark. I do not believe that Christopher Columbus, when he started on his rather successful voyage of discovery, felt half the responsibility and importance that weighed upon me as I sat on the middle seat of the Dolphin, with my oar resting in the row-lock. I wonder if Christopher Columbus quietly slipped out of the house without letting his estimable family know what he was up to? Charley Harden, whose father had promised to cane him if he ever stepped foot on sail or row boat, came down to the wharf in a sour-grape humor, to see us off. Nothing would tempt him to go out on the river in such a crazy clam-shell of a boat. He pretended that he did not expect to behold us alive again, and tried to throw a wet blanket over the expedition.

" Guess you '11 have a squally time of it," said Charley, casting off the painter. " I '11 drop in at

old Newbury's " (Newbury was the parish under-taker) " and leave word, as I go along!'

"Bosh!" muttered Phil Adams, sticking the boat-hook into the string-piece of the wharf, and sending the Dolphin half a dozen yards towards the current.

How calm and lovely the river was! Not a ripple stirred on the glassy surface, broken only by the sharp cutwater of our tiny craft. The sun, as round and red as an August moon, was by thistime peering above the water-line.

The town had drifted behind us, and we wereentering among the group of islands. Sometimeswe could almost touch with our boat-hook theshelving banks on either side. As we neared themouth of the harbor, a little breeze now and thenwrinkled the blue water, shook the spangles fromthe foliage, and gently lifted the spiral mist-wreaths that still clung along shore. The meas-ured dip of our oars and the drowsy twitterings ofthe birds seemed to mingle with, rather than break,the enchanted silence that reigned about us.

The scent of the new clover comes back to menow, as I recall that delicious morning when wefloated away in a fairy boat down a river like adream!

The sun was well up when the nose of the Dol-phin nestled against the snow-white bosom ofSandpeep Island. This island, as I have saidbefore, was the last of the cluster, one side of it

On Sandpeep Island

being washed by the sea. We landed on theriver side, the sloping sands and quiet water af-fording us a good place to moor the boat.

It took us an hour or more to transport ourstores to the spot selected for the encampment.Having pitched our tent, using the five oars tosupport the canvas, we got out our lines, and went down the rocks seaward to fish. It was early for cunners, but we were lucky enough to catch as nice a mess as ever you saw. A cod for the chowder was not so easily secured. At last Binny Wallace hauled in a plump little fellow crusted all over with flaky silver.

To skin the fish, build our fireplace, and cook the chowder, kept us busy the next two hours.

The fresh air and the exercise had given us the appetites of wolves, and we were about famished by the time the savory mixture was ready for our clam-shell saucers.

I shall not insult the rising generation on the seaboard by telling them how delectable is a chowder compounded and eaten in this Robinson Crusoe fashion. As for the boys who live inland, and know naught of such marine feasts, my heart is full of pity for them. What wasted lives! Not to know the delights of a clam-bake, not to love chowder, to be ignorant of lob-scouse !

How happy we were, we four, sitting cross-legged in the crisp salt grass, with the invigorat-ing sea-breeze blowing gratefully through our hair! What a joyous thing was life, and how far off seemed death — death, that lurks in all pleasant places, and was so near!

The banquet finished, Phil Adams drew from his pocket a handful of sweet-fern cigars; but as none of the party could indulge without imminent risk of becoming ill, we all, on one pretext or an-jther, declined, and Phil smoked by himself.

The wind had freshened by this, and we found it comfortable to put on the jackets which had been thrown aside in the heat of the day. We strolled along the beach and gathered large quan-tities of the fairy-woven Iceland moss, which, at certain seasons, is washed to these shores; then we played at ducks and drakes, and then, the sun being sufficiently low, we went in bathing.

Before our bath was ended a slight change had come over the sky and sea; fleecy-white clouds scudded here and there, and a muffled moan from the breakers caught our ears from time to time. While we were dressing, a few hurried drops of rain came lisping down, and we adjourned to the tent to wait the passing of the squall.

"We're all right, anyhow," said Phil Adams." It won't be much of a blow, and we '11 be as snug as a bug in a rug, here in the tent, particu-larly if we have that lemonade which some of you fellows were going to make."

By an oversight, the lemons had been left in the boat. Binny Wallace volunteered to go for them.

" Put an extra stone on the painter, Binny," said Adams, calling after him; " it would be awk-ward to have the Dolphin give us the slip and re-turn to port minus her passengers."

" That it would," answered Binny, scrambling down the rocks.

Sandpeep Island is diamond shaped — one point running out into the sea, and the other looking to-wards the town. Our tent was on the river side. Though the Dolphin was also on the same side, it lay out of sight by the beach at the farther ex-tremity of the island.

Binny Wallace had been absent five or six minutes, when we heard him calling our several names in tones that indicated distress or surprise, we could not tell which. Our first thought was,"The boat has broken adrift!':

We sprung to our feet and hastened down to the beach. On turning the bluff which hid the mooring-place from our view, we found the con-jecture correct. Not only was the Dolphin afloat, but poor little Binny Wallace was standing in the bows with his arms stretched helplessly towards us — drifting out to sea !

" Head the boat in shore !" shouted Phil Adams.

Wallace ran to the tiller; but the slight cockle-shell merely swung round and drifted broadside on. Oh, if we had but left a single scull in the Dolphin !

" Can you swim it ?" cried Adams desperately, using his hand as a speaking-trumpet, for the dis-tance between the boat and the island widenedmomently.

Binny Wallace looked down at the sea, which wascovered with white caps, and made a despairinggesture. He knew, and we knew, that the stout-est swimmer could not live forty seconds in thoseangry waters.

A wild, insane light came into Phil Adams'seyes, as he stood knee-deep in the boiling surf,and for an instant I think he meditated plunginginto the ocean after the receding boat.

The sky darkened, and an ugly look stole rap-idly over the broken surface of the sea.

Binny Wallace half rose from his seat in thestern, and waved his hand to us in token of fare-well. In spite of the distance, increasing everyinstant, we could see his face plainly. The anx-ious expression it wore at first had passed. Itwas pale and meek now, and I love to think therewas a kind of halo about it, like that which paint-ers place around the forehead of a saint. So hedrifted away.

The sky grew darker and darker. It was onlyby straining our eyes through the unnatural twi-light that we could keep the Dolphin in sight.The figure of Binny Wallace was no longer visible,for the boat itself had dwindled to a mere whitedot on the black water. Now we lost it, and ourhearts stopped throbbing; and now the speck ap-

peared again, for an instant, on the crest of a highwave.

Finally, it went out like a spark, and we saw itno more. Then we gazed at each other, and darednot speak.

Absorbed in following the course of the boat,we had scarcely noticed the huddled inky clouds

Drifting Away

that sagged down all around us. From thesethreatening masses, seamed at intervals with palelightning, there now burst a heavy peal of thun-der that shook the ground under our feet. A sud-

den squall struck the sea, ploughing deep whitefurrows into it, and at the same instant a singlepiercing shriek rose above the tempest — thefrightened cry of a gull swooping over the island.How it startled us !

It was impossible any longer to keep our foot-ing on the beach. The wind and the breakerswould have swept us into the ocean if we had notclung to each other with the desperation of drown-ing men. Taking advantage of a momentary lull,we crawled up the sands on our hands and knees,and, pausing in the lee of the granite ledge to gainbreath, returned to the camp, where we found thatthe gale had snapped all the fastenings of the tentbut one. Held by this, the puffed-out canvasswayed in the wind like a balloon. It was a taskof some difficulty to secure it, which we did bybeating down the canvas with the oars.

After several trials, we succeeded in setting upthe tent on the leeward side of the ledge. Blindedby the vivid flashes of lightning, and drenched bythe rain, which fell in torrents, we crept, half deadwith fear and anguish, under our flimsy shelter.Neither the anguish nor the fear was on our ownaccount, for we were comparatively safe, but forpoor little Binny Wallace, driven out to sea in themerciless gale. We shuddered to think of him inthat frail shell, drifting on and on to his grave,the sky rent with lightning over his head, and thegreen abysses yawning beneath him. We fell to

crying, the three of us, and cried I know not howlong.

Meanwhile the storm raged with augmentedfury. We were obliged to hold on to the ropes ofthe tent to prevent it blowing away. The sprayfrom the river leaped several yards up the rocksand clutched at us malignantly. The very islandtrembled with the concussions of the sea beatingupon it, and at times I fancied that it had brokenloose from its foundation, and was floating offwith us. The breakers, streaked with angry phos-phorus, were fearful to look at.

The wind rose higher and higher, cutting longslits in the tent, through which the rain pouredincessantly. To complete the sum of our miseries,the night was at hand. It came down suddenly,at last, like a curtain, shutting in Sandpeep Islandfrom all the world.

It was a dirty night, as the sailors say. Thedarkness was something that could be felt as wellas seen—it pressed down upon one with a cold,clammy touch. Gazing into the hollow blackness,all sorts of imaginable shapes seemed to startforth from vacancy— brilliant colors, stars, prisms,and dancing lights. What boy, lying awake atnight, has not amused or terrified himself by peo«pling the spaces around his bed with these phe-nomena of his own eyes ?

" I say," whispered Fred Langdon, at length,clutching my hand, " don't you see things — outthere — in the dark ?"

" Yes, yes — Binny Wallace's face !'

I added to my own nervousness by making thisavowal; though for the last ten minutes I had seenlittle besides that star-pale face with its angelichair and brows. First a slim yellow circle, likethe nimbus round the moon, took shape and grewsharp against the darkness; then this faded grad-ually, and there was the Face, wearing the samesad, sweet look it wore when he waved his hand tous across the awful water. This optical illusionkept repeating itself.

"And I too," said Adams. " I see it every nowand then, outside there. What would n't I give ifit really was poor little Wallace looking in at us!O boys, how shall we dare to go back to the townwithout htm ? I 've wished a hundred times, sincewe 've been sitting here, that I was in his place,alive or dead !"

We dreaded the approach of morning as muchas we longed for it. The morning would tell usall. Was it possible for the Dolphin to outridesuch a storm ? There was a lighthouse on Mack-erel Reef, which lay directly in the course the boathad taken when it disappeared. If the Dolphinhad caught on this reef, perhaps Binny Wallacewas safe. Perhaps his cries had been heard by thekeeper of the light. The man owned a life-boat,and had rescued several persons. Who could tell ?

Such were the questions we asked ourselvesagain and again, as we lay in each other's arms

waiting for daybreak. What an endless night itwas ! I have known months that did not seem solong.

Our position was irksome rather than perilous ;for the day was certain to bring us relief from thetown, where our prolonged absence, together withthe storm, had no doubt excited the liveliest alarmfor our safety. But the cold, the darkness, andthe suspense were hard to bear.

Our soaked jackets had chilled us to the bone.To keep warm, we lay huddled together so closelythat we could hear our hearts beat above the tu-mult of sea and sky.

After a while we grew very hungry, not havingbroken our fast since early in the day. The rainhad turned the hard-tack into a sort of dough; butit was better than nothing.

We used to laugh at Fred Langdon for alwayscarrying in his pocket a small vial of essence ofpeppermint or sassafras, a few drops of which,sprinkled on a lump of loaf-sugar, he seemed toconsider a great luxury. I do not know whatwould have become of us at this crisis if it hadnot been for that omnipresent bottle of hot stuff.We poured the stinging liquid over our sugar,which had kept dry in a sardine-box, and warmedourselves with frequent doses.

After four or five hours the rain ceased, thewind died away to a moan, and the sea — nolonger raging like a maniac — sobbed and sobbed

with a piteous human voice all along the coast.And well it might, after that night's work.Twelve sail of the Gloucester fishing fleet hadgone down with every soul on board, just outsideof Whale's-back Light. Think of the wide griefthat follows in the wake of one wreck; then thinkof the despairing women who wrung their handsand wept, the next morning, in the streets ofGloucester, Marblehead, and Newcastle!

Though our strength was nearly spent, we weretoo cold to sleep. Once I sunk into a troubleddoze, when I seemed to hear Charley Marden'sparting words, only it was the Sea that said them.After that I threw off the drowsiness whenever itthreatened to overcome me.

Fred Langdon was the earliest to discover afilmy, luminous streak in the sky, the first glim-mering of sunrise.

" Look, it is nearly daybreak! '

While we were following the direction of hisfinger, a sound of distant oars fell upon our ears.

We listened breathlessly, and as the dip of theblades became more audible, we discerned twofoggy lights, like will-o'-the-wisps, floating on theriver.

Running down to the water's edge, we hailedthe boats with all our might. The call was heard,for the oars rested a moment in the row-locks, andthen pulled in towards the island.

It was two boats from the town, in the foremost of which we could now make out the figures ofCaptain Nutter and Binny Wallace's father. Weshrunk back on seeing him.

" Thank God ! " cried Mr. Wallace fervently, ashe leaped from the wherry without waiting for thebow to touch the beach.

But when he saw only three boys standing onthe sands, his eye wandered restlessly about inquest of the fourth ; then a deadly pallor over-spread his features.

Our story was soon told. A solemn silence fellupon the crowd of rough boatmen gathered round,interrupted only by a stifled sob from one poor oldman, who stood apart from the rest.

The sea was still running too high for any smallboat to venture out; so it was arranged that thewherry should take us back to town, leaving theyawl, with a picked crew, to hug the island untildaybreak, and then set forth in search of the Dol-phin.

Though it was barely sunrise when we reachedtown, there were a great many persons assembledat the landing eager for intelligence from missingboats. Two picnic parties had started down riverthe day before, just previous to the gale, and no-thing had been heard of them. It turned out thatthe pleasure-seekers saw their danger in time, andran ashore on one of the least exposed islands,where they passed the night. Shortly after ourown arrival they appeared off Rivermouth, much

to the joy of their friends, in two shattered, dis-masted boats.

The excitement over, I was in a forlorn state,physically and mentally. Captain Nutter put meto bed between hot blankets, and sent Kitty Col-lins for the doctor. I was wandering in my mind,and fancied myself still on Sandpeep Island: nowwe were building our brick stove to cook the chow-der, and, in my delirium, I laughed aloud andshouted to my comrades; now the sky darkened,and the squall struck the island; now I gaveorders to Wallace how to manage the boat, andnow I cried because the rain was pouring in onme through the holes in the tent. Towards even-ing a high fever set in, and it was many days be-fore my grandfather deemed it prudent to tell methat the Dolphin had been found, floating keel up-wards, four miles southeast of Mackerel Reef.

Poor little Binny Wallace! How strange itseemed, when I went to school again, to see thatempty seat in the fifth row ! How gloomy the play-ground was, lacking the sunshine of his gentle,sensitive face! One day a folded sheet slippedfrom my algebra; it was the last note he everwrote me. I could not read it for the tears.

What a pang shot across my heart the after-noon it was whispered through the town that abody had been washed ashore at Grave Point —the place where we bathed. We bathed there nomore! How well I remember the funeral, and

what a piteous sight it was afterwards to see hisfamiliar name on a small headstone in the OldSouth Burying Ground !

Poor little Binny Wallace! Always the sameto me. The rest of us have grown up into hard,worldly men, fighting the fight of life; but you areforever young, and gentle, and pure ; a part of myown childhood that time cannot wither; always alittle boy, always poor little Binny Wallace!

CHAPTER XV

AN OLD ACQUAINTANCE TURNS UP

A YEAR had stolen by since the death of BinnyWallace — a year of which I have nothing impor-tant to record.

The loss of our little playmate threw a shadowover our young lives for many and many a month.The Dolphin rose and fell with the tide at the footof the slippery steps, unused, the rest of the sum-mer. At the close of November we hauled hersadly into the boathouse for the winter ; but whenspring came round we launched the Dolphin again,and often went down to the wharf and looked ather lying in the tangled eel^rass, without muchinclination to take a row. The associations con-nected with the boat were too painful as yet;but time, which wears the sharp edge from every-thing, softened this feeling, and one afternoon webrought out the cobwebbed oars.

The ice once broken, brief trips along thewharves — we seldom cared to go out into theriver now — became one of our chief amusements.Meanwhile Gypsy was not forgotten. Every clearmorning I was in the saddle before breakfast, andthere are few roads or lanes within ten miles of

Rivermouth that have not borne the print of hervagrant hoof.

I studied like a good fellow this quarter, carry-ing off a couple of first prizes. The Captain ex-pressed his gratification by presenting me witha new silver dollar. If a dollar in his eyes wassmaller than a cart-wheel, it was not so very muchsmaller. I redeemed my pencil-case from thetreasurer of the Centipedes, and felt that I wasgetting on in the world

It was at this time I was greatly cast down bya letter from my father saying that he should beunable to visit Rivermouth until the followingyear. With that letter came another to CaptainNutter, which he did not read aloud to the fam-ily, as usual. It was on business, he said, foldingit up in his wallet. He received several of thesebusiness letters from time to time, and I noticedthat they always made him silent and moody.

The fact is my father's banking-house was notthriving. The unlooked-for failure of a firm largelyindebted to him had crippled "the house." Whenthe Captain imparted this information to me I didnot trouble myself over the matter. I supposed —if I supposed anything — that all grown-up peoplehad more or less money, when they wanted it.Whether they inherited it, or whether governmentsupplied them, was not clear to me. A loose ideathat my father had a private gold-mine somewhereor other relieved me of all uneasiness.

I was not far from right. Every man has withinhimself a gold-mine whose riches are limited onlyby his own industry. It is true, it sometimeshappens that industry does not avail, if a manlacks that something which, for want of a bettername, we call luck. My father was a person ofuntiring energy and ability ; but he had no luck.To use a Rivermouth saying, he was alwayscatching sculpins when every one else with thesame bait was catching mackerel.

It was more than two years since I had seenmy parents. I felt that I could not bear a longerseparation. Every letter from New Orleans — wegot two or three a month — gave me a fit of home-sickness ; and when it was definitely settled thatmy father and mother were to remain in the Southanother twelvemonth, I resolved to go to them.

Since Binny Wallace's death, Pepper Whitcombhad been my fidus Achates; we occupied desksnear each other at school, and were always to-gether in play hours. We rigged a twine telegraphfrom his garret window to the scuttle of the Nut-ter House, and sent messages to each other in amatch-box. We shared our pocket-money and oursecrets — those amazing secrets which boys have.We met in lonely places by stealth, and parted likeconspirators; we could not buy a jackknife or builda kite without throwing an air of mystery andguilt over the transaction.

I naturally hastened to lay my New Orleans

project before Pepper Whitcomb, having draggedhim for that purpose to a secluded spot in thedark pine woods outside the town. Pepper lis-tened to me with a gravity which he will not be

The Telegraph

able to surpass when he becomes Chief Justice,and strongly advised me to go.

"The summer vacation," said Pepper, "lastssix weeks ; that will give you a fortnight to spendin New Orleans, allowing two weeks each way forthe journey."

I wrung his hand and begged him to accompanyme, offering to defray all the expenses. I was no-thing if I was not princely in those days. Afterconsiderable urging, he consented to go on termsso liberal. The whole thing was arranged ; therewas nothing to do now but to advise Captain Nut-ter of my plan, which I did the next day.

The possibility that he might oppose the tournever entered my head. I was therefore totallyunprepared for the vigorous negative which metmy proposal. I was deeply mortified, moreover,for there was Pepper Whitcomb on the wharf, atthe foot of the street, waiting for me to come andlet him know what day we were to start.

" Go to New Orleans ? Go to Jericho!" ex-claimed Captain Nutter. " You 'd look pretty, youtwo, philandering off, like the babes in the wood,twenty-five hundred miles, 'with all the world be-fore you where to choose'!"

And the Captain's features, which had worn anindignant air as he began the sentence, relaxedinto a broad smile. Whether it was at the felicityof his own quotation, or at the mental picture hedrew of Pepper and myself on our travels, I couldnot tell, and little cared. I was heart-broken.How could I face my chum after all the dazzlinginducements I had held out to him ?

My grandfather, seeing that I took the matterseriously, pointed out the difficulties of such ajourney and the great expense involved. He en-tered into the details of my father's money trou-bles, and succeeded in making it plain to me thatmy wishes, under the circumstances, were some-what unreasonable. It was in no cheerful moodthat I joined Pepper at the end of the wharf.

I found that young gentleman leaning againstthe bulkhead gazing intently towards the islands

in the harbor. He had formed a telescope of hishands, and was so occupied with his observationsas to be oblivious of my approach.

" Hullo !" cried Pepper, dropping his hands."Look there ! is n't that a bark coming up theNarrows ?'

"Where?"

"Just at the left of Fishcrate Island. Don'tyou see the foremast peeping above the old der-rick?"

Sure enough, it was a vessel of considerable size,slowly beating up to town. In a few momentsmore the other two masts were visible above thegreen hillocks.

" Fore-topmasts blown away," said Pepper." Putting in for repairs, I guess."

As the bark lazily crept from behind the last ofthe islands, she let go her anchors and swunground with the tide. Then the gleeful chant ofthe sailors at the capstan came to us pleasantlyacross the water. The vessel lay within threequarters of a mile of us, and we could plainly seethe men at the davits lowering the starboardlong-boat. It no sooner touched the stream thana dozen of the crew scrambled like mice over theside of the merchantman.

In a neglected seaport like Rivermouth the ar-rival of a large ship is an event of moment. Theprospect of having twenty or thirty jolly tars letloose on the peaceful town excites divers emo-

tions among the inhabitants. The small shop-keepers along the wharves anticipate a thrivingtrade; the proprietors of the two rival boarding-houses— the "Wee Drop " and the "Mariner'sHome" — hasten down to the landing to securelodgers; and the female population of AnchorLane turn out to a woman, for a ship fresh fromsea is always full of possible husbands and long-lost prodigal sons.

But aside from this there is scant welcomegiven to a ship's crew in Rivermouth. The toil-worn mariner is asad fellow ashore, judging him bya severe moralstandard.

Once, I re-member, a Unit-ed States frigatecame into port forrepairs after astorm. She lay!l in the river a fort-night or more,and every daysent us a gang of sixty or seventy of our country'sgallant defenders, who spread themselves over thetown, doing all sorts of mad things. They weregood-natured enough, but full of old Sancho.The " Wee Drop" proved a drop too much for

A Midnight Call

many of them. They went singing through thestreets at midnight, wringing off door-knockers,shinning up water-spouts, and frightening the Old-est Inhabitant nearly to death by popping theirheads into his second-story window, and shouting" Fire ! " One morning a blue-jacket was discov-ered in a perilous plight, half way up the steepleof the South Church, clinging to the lightning-rod.How he got there nobody could tell, not even blue-jacket himself. All he knew was, that the leg ofhis trousers had caught on a nail, and there hestuck, unable to move either way. It cost thetown five or six dollars to get him down again. Hedirected the workmen how to splice the laddersbrought to his assistance, and called his rescuers"butter-fingered land-lubbers" with delicious cool-ness.

But those were man-of-war's men. The sedate-looking craft now lying off Fish crate Island wasnot likely to carry any such lively cargo. Never-theless, we watched the coming in of the long-boat with considerable interest.

As it drew near, the figure of the man pullingthe bow-oar seemed oddly familiar to me. Wherecould I have seen him before ? When and where ?His back was towards me, but there was some-thing about that closely cropped head that I rec-ognized instantly.

" Way enough !' cried the steersman, and allthe oars stood upright in the air. The man in the bow seized the boat-hook, and, turning roundquickly, showed me the honest face of Sailor Benof the Typhoon.

" It's Sailor Ben ! " I cried, nearly pushing Pep-per Whitcomb overboard in my excitement.

Sailor Ben, with the wonderful pink lady on hisarm, and the ships and stars and anchors tattooedall over him, was a well-known hero among myplaymates. And there he was, like something ina dream come true !

I did not wait for my old acquaintance to getfirmly on the wharf, before I grasped his hand inboth of mine.

" Sailor Ben, don't you remember me ?"

He evidently did not. He shifted his quidfrom one cheek to the other, and looked at memeditatively.

" Lord love ye, lad, I don't know you. I wasnever here afore in my life."

" What!' I cried, enjoying his perplexity,"have you forgotten the voyage from New Orleans in the Typhoon, two years ago, you lovelyold picture-book ?'

Ah ! then he knew me, and in token of the rec-ollection gave my hand such a squeeze that I amsure an unpleasant change came over my coun-tenance.

" Bless my eyes, but you have growed ! I shouldn't have knowed you if I had met you in Singa-pore !"

Without stopping to inquire, as I was temptedto do, why he was more likely to recognize me inSingapore than anywhere else, I invited him tocome at once up to the Nutter House, where I in-sured him a warm welcome from the Captain.

" Hold steady, Master Tom," said Sailor Ben,slipping the painter through the ringbolt and tyingthe loveliest knot you ever saw ; " hold steady tillI see if the mate can let me off. If you please,sir," he continued, addressing the steersman, avery red-faced, bow-legged person, " this here is alittle shipmate o' mine as wants to talk over backtimes along of me, if so it 's convenient."

"All right, Ben," returned the mate; "shan'twant you for an hour."

Leaving one man in charge of the boat, themate and the rest of the crew went off together.In the mean while Pepper Whitcomb had got outhis cunner line, and was quietly fishing at the endof the wharf, as if to give me the idea that he wasnot very much impressed by my intimacy with sorenowned a character as Sailor Ben. PerhapsPepper was a little jealous. At any rate, he re-fused to go with us to the house.

Captain Nutter was at home reading the River-mouth Barnacle. He was a reader to do an editor'sheart good; he never skipped over an advertise-ment, even if he had read it fifty times before.Then the paper went the rounds of the neighbor-hood, among the poor people, like the single port-

able eye which the three blind crones passed toeach other in the legend of King Acrisius. TheCaptain, I repeat, was wandering in the labyrinthsof the Rivermouth Barnacle when I led Sailor Beninto the sitting-room.

My grandfather, whose inborn courtesy knewj no distinctions, received my nautical friend as ifhe had been an admiral instead of a common fore-castle-hand. Sailor Ben pulled an imaginary tuftof hair on his forehead, and bowed clumsily. Sail-ors have a way of using their forelock as a sort ofhandle to bow with.

The old tar had probably never been in so hand-some an apartment in all his days, and nothingcould induce him to take the inviting mahoganychair which the Captain wheeled out from the cor-ner.

The abashed mariner stood up against the wall,twirling his tarpaulin in his two hands and lookingextremely silly. He made a poor show in a gen-tleman's drawing-room, but what a fellow he hadbeen in his day, when the gale blew great gunsand the topsails wanted reefing! I thought ofhim with the Mexican squadron off Vera Cruz,where

" The rushing battle-bolt sung from the three-decker out of thefoam,"

and he did not seem awkward or ignoble to me, forall his shyness.

As Sailor Ben declined to sit down, the Captain

did not resume his seat; so we three stood in aconstrained manner until my grandfather went tothe door and called to Kitty to bring in a decan-ter of madeira and two glasses.

" My grandson, here, has talked so much about

Introducing Sailor Ben

you," said the Captain pleasantly, "that you seem^quite like an old acquaintance to me."

" Thankee, sir, thankee," returned Sailor Ben,looking as guilty as if he had been detected inpicking a pocket.

"And I 'm very glad to see you, Mr. —Mr. —*

"Watson — Benjamin Watson."

" Mr. Watson," added the Captain. " Tom, openthe door, there 's Kitty with the glasses."

I opened the door, and Kitty entered the roombringing the things on a waiter, which she wasabout to set on the table, when suddenly she ut-tered a loud shriek; the decanter and glasses fellwith a crash to the floor, and Kitty, as white as asheet, was seen flying through the hall.

" It's his wraith ! It's his wraith l! " we heardKitty shrieking, in the kitchen.

My grandfather and I turned with amazementto Sailor Ben. His eyes were standing out of hishead like a lobster's.

" It's my own little Irish lass !' shouted thesailor, and he darted into the hall after her.

Even then we scarcely caught the meaning ofhis words, but when we saw Watson and Kittysobbing on each other's shoulder in the kitchen,we understood it all.

" I begs your honor's parden, sir," he said, lift-ing his tear-stained face above Kitty's tumbledhair ; " I begs your honor's parden for kicking upa rumpus in the house, but it's my own littleIrish lass as I lost so long ago !"

" Heaven preserve us ! " cried the Captain, blow-ing his nose violently — a transparent ruse to hidehis emotion.

1 Ghost, spirit.

AN OLD ACQUAINTANCE TURNS UP 19*

Miss Abigail was in an upper chamber, sweeping ; but on hearing the unusual racket below, shescented an accident and came ambling downstairswith a bottle of the infallible hot-drops in her hand.Nothing but the firmness of my grandfather pre-vented her from giving Sailor Ben a tablespoon-ful on the spot. But when she learned what hadcome about — that this was Kitty's husband, thatKitty Collins was not Kitty Collins now, but Mrs.Benjamin Watson of Nantucket —the good soulsat down on the meal-chest and sobbed as if—toquote from Captain

Nutter — as if a husband of her own had turned up !

A happier set of persons than we were never met together in a dingy kitchen or anywhere else. The Captain ordered a fresh decanter of madeira, and made all hands, excepting myself, drink a cup to the return of " the prodigal sea-son," as he called Sailor Ben.

After the first flush of joy and surprise was over, Kitty grew silent and constrained. Now and then she fixed her eyes thoughtfully on her husband. Why had he deserted her all these long years ? What right had he to look for a welcome from one he had treated so cruelly ? She had been true to him, but had he been true to her ? Sailor Ben must have guessed what was passing in her mind, for presently he took her hand and said, —

" Well, lass, it's a long yarn, but you shall have it all in good time. It was my hard luck as made

us part company, an' no will of mine, for I loved you dear."

Kitty brightened up immediately, needing no other assurance of Sailor Ben's faithfulness.

When his hour had expired, we walked with him down to the wharf, where the Captain held a consultation with the mate, which resulted in an extension of Mr. Watson's leave of absence, and afterwards in his discharge from his ship. We then went to the " Mariner's Home " to engage a room for him, as he would not hear of accepting the hospitalities of the Nutter House.

" You see, I 'm only an uneddicated man," he remarked to my grandfather, by way of explana-tion.

CHAPTER XVI

IN WHICH SAILOR BEN SPINS A YARN

OF course we were all very curious to learn what had befallen Sailor Ben that morning long ago, when he bade his little bride good-by and disap-peared so mysteriously.

After tea, that same evening, we assembled around the table in the kitchen — the only place where Sailor Ben felt at home — to hear what he had to say for himself.

The candles were snuffed, and a pitcher of foam-ing nut-brown ale was set at the elbow of the speaker, who was evidently embarrassed by the re-spectability of his audience, consisting of Captain Nutter, Miss Abigail, myself, and Kitty, whose face shone with happiness like one of the pol-ished tin platters on the dresser.

"Well, my hearties," commenced Sailor Ben —then he stopped short and turned very red, as it struck him that maybe this was not quite the proper way to address a dignitary like the Captain and a severe elderly lady like Miss Abigail Nutter, who sat bolt upright staring at him as she would have stared at the Tycoon of Japan himself.

" I ain't much of a hand at spinnin' a yarn,"

remarked Sailor Ben, apologetically, " 'specially when the yarn is all about a man as has made a fool of hisself, an' 'specially when that man's name is Benjamin Watson."

" Bravo ! " cried Captain Nutter, rapping on the table encouragingly.

"Thankee, sir, thankee. I go back to the time when Kitty an' me was livin* in lodgin's by the dock in New York. We was as happy, sir, as two porpusses, which they toil not neither do they spin. But when I seed the money gittin' low in the locker — Kitty's starboard stockin', savin' your presence, marm — I got down-hearted like, seein' as I should be obleeged to skip agin, for it did n't seem as I could do much ashore. An' then the sea was my nat'ral spear of action. I was n't ex-actly born on it, look you, but I fell into it the fust time I was let out arter my birth. My mother slipped her cable for a heavenly port afore I was old enough to hail her; so I larnt to look on the ocean for a sort of stepmother — an' a precious hard one she has been to me.

"The idee of leavin' Kitty so soon arter our marriage went agin my grain considerable. I cruised along the docks for somethin' to do in the way of stevedore ; an' though I picked up a strayjob here and there, I did n't arn enough to buyship-bisket for a rat, let alone feedin' two humanmouths. There was n't nothin' honest I would n'thave turned a hand to ; but the 'longshoremen

gobbled up all the work, an' a outsider like medid n't stand a show.

" Things got from bad to worse ; the month'srent took all our cash except a dollar or so, an' thesky looked kind o' squally fore an' aft. Well, Iset out one mornin' — that identical unlucky morn-in'— determined to come back an' toss some payinto Kitty's lap, if I had to sell my jacket for it.I spied a brig unloadin' coal at pier No. 47 — howwell I remembers it! I hailed the mate, an* of-fered myself for a coal-heaver. But I was n'twanted, as he told me civilly enough, which wasbetter treatment than usual. As I turned offrather glum I was signaled by one of them sleek,smooth-spoken rascals with a white hat an' a weedon it, as is always goin' about the piers a-seekin'who they may devower.

" We sailors know 'em for rascals from stem tostarn, but somehow every fresh one fleeces us jestas his mate did afore him. We don't larn nothin'by exper'ence; we 're jest no better than a lot ofbabbys with no brains.

" ' Good-mornin', my man/ sez the chap, as ileyas you please.

" ' Mornin', sir/ sez I.

" ' Lookin' for a job ?' sez he.

" 'Through the big end of a telescope/ sez I —meanin' that the chances for a job looked verysmall from my pint of view.

"'You 're the man for my money/ sez he

smilin* as innocent as a cherubim; 'jest step inhere, till we talk it over.'

" So I goes with him like a nat'ral-born idiot,into a little grocery-shop near by, where we setsdown at a table with a bottle atween us. Then itcomes out as there is a New Bedford whaler ab mt

" Lookin" for a job?"

to start for the fishin' grounds, an' jest one able-bodied sailor like me is wanted to make up thecrew. Would I go ? Yes, I would n't on noterms.

" ' I bet you fifty dollars,' sez he, ' that you 11come back fust mate.'

"'I bet you a hundred/ sez I, 'that I don't,

for I 've signed papers as keeps me ashore, an' theparson has witnessed the deed.'

" So we sat there, he urgin' me to ship, an' Ichaffin' him cheerful over the bottle.

"Arter a while I begun to feel a little queer;things got foggy in my upper works, an' I remem-bers, faintlike, of signin' a paper ; then I remem-bers bein' in a small boat; and then I remembersnothin' until I heard the mate's whistle pipin*all hands on deck. I tumbled up with the rest,an' there I was — on board of a whaler outwardbound for a three years' cruise, an' my dear littlelass ashore awaitin' for me."

" Miserable wretch!' said Miss Abigail, in avoice that vibrated among the tin platters on thedresser. This was Miss Abigail's way of testify-ing her sympathy.

"Thankee, marm," returned Sailor Ben doubt-fully.

" No talking to the man at the wheel," crie theCaptain. Upon which we all laughed. " Spm I"added my grandfather.

Sailor Ben resumed : —

" I leave you to guess the wretchedness as fellupon me, for I 've not got the gift to tell you.There I was down on the ship's books for a threeyears' viage, an' no help for it. I feel nigh to sixhundred years old when I think how long thatviage was. There is n't no hour-glass as runs slowenough to keep a tally of the slowns^s of them

fust hours. But I done my duty like a man, seein'there was n't no way of gettin' out of it. I toldmy shipmates of the trick as had been played onme, an' they tried to cheer me up a bit; but I wassore sorrowful for a long spell. Many a night onwatch I put my face in my hands and sobbed forthinkin' of the little woman left among the land'sharks, an' no man to have an eye on her, Godbless her!"

Here Kitty softly drew her chair nearer toSailor Ben, and rested one hand on his arm.

" Our adventures among the whales, I take it,does n't consarn the present company here assem-bled. So I give that the go by. There 's an endto everythin', even to a whalin' viage. My heartall but choked me the day we put into New Bed-ford with our cargo of ile. I got my three years'pay in a lump, an* made for New York like aflash of lightnin'. The people hove to and lookedat me, as I rushed through the streets like a mad-man, until I came to the spot where the lodgin'-house stood on West Street. But, Lord love ye,there was no sech lodgin'-house there, but a greatnew brick shop.

" I made bold to go in an' ask arter the oldplace, but nobody knowed nothin' about it, save asit had been torn down two years or more. I wasadrift now, for I had reckoned all them days andnights on gittin' word of Kitty from Dan Shack-ford, the man as kept the lodgin'.

"As I stood there with all the wind knockedout of my sails, the idee of runnin' alongside theperlice-station popped into my head. The perlicewas likely to know the latitude of a man like Dan

Settling the Land Shark's Account

Shackford who was n't over an* above respeck-tible. They did know — he had died in theTombs jail that day twelvemonth. A coincy-dunce, was n't it ? I was ready to drop whenthey told me this ; howsomever, I bore up an' givethe chief a notion of the fix I was in. He writ anotice which I put into the newspapers every day

for three months; but nothin' come of it. Icruised over the city week in and week out; Iwent to every sort of place where they hired wo-men hands ; I did n't leave a think undone thata uneddicated man could do. But nothin' comeof it. I don't believe there was a wretchedersoul in that big city of wretchedness than me.Sometimes I wanted to lay down in the streetsand die.

" Driftin' disconsolate one day among the ship-pin', who should I overhaul but the identicalsmooth-spoken chap with a white hat an' a weedon it! I did n't know if there was any sperit leftin me, till I clapped eye on his very onpleasantcountenance. 'You villain!' sez I, ' where's mylittle Irish lass as you dragged me away from ?'an' I lighted on him, hat and all, like that!'

Here Sailor Ben brought his fist down on thedeal table with the force of a sledge-hammer.Miss Abigail gave a start, and the ale leaped upin the pitcher like a miniature fountain.

" I begs your parden, ladies and gentlemen;but the thought of that feller with his ring an'his watch-chain an' his walrus face is alus toomany for me. I was for pitchin' him into theNorth River, when a perliceman prevented mefrom benefitin' the human family. I had to payfive - dollars for hitin' the chap (they said it was saltand buttery), an' that 's what I call a neat, genteelluxury. It was worth double the money jest to

see that white hat, with a weed on it, lay in' on thewharf like a busted accordiun.

" Arter months of useless sarch, I went to seaagin. I never got into a foren port but I kept awatch out for Kitty. Once I thought I seed herin Liverpool, but it was only a gal as looked likeher. The numbers of women in different parts ofthe world as looked like her was amazin'. So agood many years crawled by, an' I wandered fromplace to place, never givin' up the sarch. I mighthave been chief mate scores of times, maybemaster; but I had n't no ambition. I seed manystrange things in them years — outlandish peoplean* cities, storms, shipwracks, an* battles. I seedmany a true mate go down, an' sometimes I en-vied them what went to their rest. But thesethings is neither here nor there.

" About a year ago I shipped on board the Bel-phoebe yonder, an' of all the strange winds as everblowed, the strangest an' the best was the windas blowed me to this here blessed spot. I can't betoo thankful. That I 'm as thankful as it is pos-sible for an uneddicated man to be, He knows asreads the heart of all."

Here ended Sailor Ben's yarn, which I havewritten down in his own homely words as nearlyas I can recall them. After he had finished, theCaptain shook hands with him and served out theale.

As Kitty was about to drink, she paused, rested the cup on her knee, and asked what day of themonth it was.

"The twenty-seventh," said the Captain, won-dering what she was driving at.

" Then," cried Kitty, " it's ten years and a daythis night since " —

" Since what ? " asked my grandfather.

" Sence the little woman and I got spliced!ncried Sailor Ben. " There *s another coincyduncefor you, if you 're wanting anything in that line."

On hearing this we all clapped hands, and theCaptain, with a degree of ceremony that was al-most painful, drank a bumper to the health andhappiness of the bride and bridegroom.

It was a pleasant sight to see the two old loverssitting side by side, in spite of all, drinking fromthe same little cup — a battered zinc dipper whichSailor Ben had un slung from a strap round hiswaist. I think I never saw him without this dip-per and a sheath-knife suspended just back of hiship, ready for any convivial occasion.

We had a merry time of it. The Captain wasin great force this evening, and not only related hisfamous exploit in the war of 1812, but regaled thecompany with a dashing sea-song from Mr. Shake-speare's play of The Tempest. My grandfather— however it came about — was a great reader ofShakespeare. He had a mellow tenor voice (notShakespeare, but the Captain), and rolled out theverse with a will:

* The master, the swabber, the boatswain, and I,

The gunner, and his mate,Lov'd Mall, Meg, and Marian, and Margery,But none of us car'd for Kate."

" A very good song, and very well sung," saysSailor Ben; " but some of us does care for Kate.Is this Mr. Shawkspear a sea-farm' man, sir ?'

" Not at present," replied the Captain, with amonstrous twinkle in his eye.

The clock was striking ten when the partybroke up. The Captain walked to the " Mariner'sHome' with his guest, in order to question himregarding his future movements.

" Well, sir," said he, " I ain't as young as I was,an; I don't cal'ulate to go to sea no more. I pro-poses to drop anchor here, an' hug the land untilthe old hulk goes to pieces. I Ve got two orthree thousand dollars in the locker, an' expectsto get on uncommon comfortable without askin*no odds from the Assylum for Decayed Mariners."

My grandfather indorsed the plan warmly, andBenjamin Watson did drop anchor in Rivermouth,where he speedily became one of the institutions ofthe town.

His first step was to buy a small one-story cot-tage located at the head of the wharf, within gun-shot of the Nutter House. To the great amuse-ment of my grandfather, Sailor Ben painted thecottage a light sky-blue, and ran a broad blackstripe around it just under the eaves. In this

stripe he painted white port-holes, at regular dis-tances, making his residence look as much like aman-of-war as possible. With a short flagstaff pro-jecting over the door like a bowsprit, the effectwas quite magical. My description of the exte-rior of this palatial residence is complete when Iadd that the proprietor nailed a horseshoe againstthe front door to keep off the witches — a verynecessary precaution in these latitudes.

The inside of Sailor Ben's abode was not lessstriking than the outside. The cottage containedtwo rooms; the one opening on the wharf hecalled his cabin ; here he ate and slept. His fewtumblers and a frugal collection of crockery wereset in a rack suspended over the table, which hada cleat of wood nailed round the edge to preventthe dishes from sliding off in case of a heavy sea.Hanging against the walls were three or fourhighly colored prints of celebrated frigates, and alithograph picture of a rosy young woman insuffi-ciently clad in the American flag. This was la-beled "Kitty," though I am sure it looked nomore like her than I did. A walrus-tooth with anEsquimau engraved on it, a shark's jaw, and theblade of a swordfish were among the enviable dec-orations of this apartment. In one corner stoodhis bunk, or bed, and in the other his well-wornsea-chest, a perfect Pandora's box of mysteries.You would have thought yourself in the cabin ofa real ship.

In the Cabin.

The little room aft, separated from the cabin by a sliding door, was the caboose. It held a cook-ing-stove, pots, pans, and groceries ; also a lot of fishing-lines and coils of tarred twine, which made the place smell like a forecastle, and a delightful smell it is — to those who fancy it.

Kitty did not leave our service, but played house-keeper for both establishments, returning at night to Sailor Ben's. He shortly added a wherry to his worldly goods, and in the fishing season made a very handsome income. During the winter he employed himself manufacturing crab-nets, for which he found no lack of customers.

His popularity among the boys was immense. A jackknife in his expert hand was a whole chest of tools. He could whittle out anything from a wooden chain to a Chinese pagoda, or a full-rigged seventy-four a foot long. To own a ship of Sailor Ben's building was to be exalted above your fellow-creatures. He did not carve many, and those he refused to sell, choosing to present them to his young friends, of whom Tom Bailey, you may be sure, was one.

How delightful it was of winter nights to sit in his cosy cabin, close to the ship's stove (he would never hear of having a fireplace), and listen to Sailor Ben's yarns! In the early summer twi-lights, when he sat on the door-step splicing a rope or mending a net, he always had a bevy of blooming young faces alongside.

The dear old fellow! How tenderly the years touched him after this ! — all the more tenderly, it seemed, for having roughed him so cruelly in other days.

CHAPTER XVII

HOW WE ASTONISHED RIVERMOUTH

SAILOR BEN'S arrival partly drove the New Or-leans project from my brain. Besides, there was just then a certain movement on foot by the Cen-tipede Club which helped to engross my attention.

Pepper Whitcomb took the Captain's veto phil-osophically, observing that he thought from the first the governor would not let me go. I do not think Pepper was quite honest in that.

But to the subject in hand.

Among the few changes that have taken place in Rivermouth during the past twenty years there is one which I regret. I lament the removal of all those varnished iron cannon which used to do duty as posts at the corners of streets leading from the river. They were quaintly ornamental, each set upon end with a solid shot soldered into its mouth, and gave to that part of the town a pic-turesqueness very poorly atoned for by the con-ventional wooden stakes that have deposed them.

These guns (" old sogers " the boys called them) had their story, like everything else in River-mouth. When that everlasting last war — the war of 1812, I mean — came to an end, all the brigs,

schooners, and barks fitted out at this port as pri-vateers were as eager to get rid of their useless twelve-pounders and swivels as they had pre-viously been to obtain them. Many of the pieces had cost large sums, and now they were little bet-ter than so much crude iron — not so good, in fact, for they were clumsy things to break up and melt over. The government did not want them; pri-vate citizens did not want them ; they were a drug in the market.

But there was one man, ridiculous beyond his generation, who got it into his head that a fortune was to be made out of these same guns. To buy them all, to hold on to them until war was declared again (as he had no doubt it would be in a few months), and then sell out at fabulous prices — this was the daring idea that addled the pate of Silas Trefethen, " Dealer in E. & W. I. Goods and Groceries," as the faded sign over his shop-door informed the public.

Silas went shrewdly to work, buying up every old cannon he could lay hands on. His back yard was soon crowded with broken-down gun-car-riages, and his barn with guns, like an arsenal.When Silas's purpose got wind it was astonishinghow valuable that thing became which just nowwas worth nothing at all.

" Ha, ha !' thought Silas ; " somebody else istryin' tu git control of the market. But I guessI 've got the start of him"

So he went on buying and buying, oftentimespaying double the original price of the article.People in the neighboring towns collected all theworthless ordnance they could find, and sent it bythe cart-load to Rivermouth.

When his barn was full, Silas began piling therubbish in his cellar, then in his parlor. Hemortgaged the stock of his grocery-store, mort-gaged his house, his barn, his horse, and wouldhave mortgaged himself if any one would havetaken him as security, in order to carry on thegranc speculation. He was a ruined man, and ashappy as a lark.

Surely poor Silas was cracked, like the majorityof his own cannon. More or less crazy he musthave been always. Years before this he pur-chased an elegant rosewood coffin, and kept it inone of the spare rooms in his residence. Heeven had his name engraved on the silver-plate,leaving a blank after the word " Died."

The blank was filled up in due time, and well itwas for Silas that he secured so stylish a coffin inhis opulent days, for when he died his worldlywealth would not have bought him a pine box, tosay nothing of rosewood. He never gave up ex-pecting a war with Great Britain. Hopeful andradiant to the last, his dying words were, England— war—few days —great profits !

It was that sweet old lady, Dame Jocelyn, whotold me the story of Silas Trefethen; for these

212 THE STORY OF A BAD BOY

things happened long before my day. Silas diedin 1817.

At Trefethen's death his unique collection cameunder the auctioneer's hammer. Some of thelarger guns were sold to the town, and planted atthe corners of divers streets; others went off tothe iron-foundry; the balance, numbering twelve,were dumped down on a deserted wharf at thefoot of Anchor Lane, where, summer after sum-mer, they rested at their ease in the grass andfungi, pelted in autumn by the rain and annu-ally buried by the winter snow. It is with thesetwelve guns that our story has to deal.

The wharf where they reposed was shut offfrom the street by a high fence — a silent, dreamyold wharf, covered with strange weeds and mosses.On account of its seclusion and the good fishingit afforded, it was much frequented by us boys.

There we met many an afternoon to throw outour lines, or play leap-frog among the rusty can-non. They were famous fellows in our eyes.What a racket they had made in the heyday oftheir unchastened youth! What stories theymight tell now, if their puffy metallic lips couldonly speak! Once they were lively talkersenough ; but there the grim sea-dogs lay, silentand forlorn in spite of all their former growlings.

They always seemed to me like a lot of vener-able disabled tars, stretched out on a lawn in frontof a hospital, gazing seaward, and mutely lament-ing their lost youth.

But once more they were destined to lift uptheir dolorous voices — once more they keeledover and lay speechless for all time. And thisis how it befell.

Jack Harris, Charley Harden, Harry Blake, andmyself were fishing off the wharf one afternoon,when a thought flashed upon me like an inspira-tion.

" I say, boys!" I cried, hauling in my line handover hand, " I Ve got something !'

" What does it pull like, youngster ?" askedHarris, looking down at the taut line and expect-ing to see a big perch at least.

" Oh, nothing in the fish way," I returned,laughing; " it's about the old guns."

" What about them ? "

" I was thinking what jolly fun it would be toset one of the old sogers on his legs and servehim out a ration of gunpowder."

Up came the three lines in a jiffy. An enter-prise better suited to the disposition of my com-panions could not have been proposed.

In a short time we had one of the smaller can-non over on its back and were busy scraping thegreen rust from the touch-hole. The mould hadspiked the gun so effectually, that for a while wefancied we should have to give up our attempt toresuscitate the old soger.

" A long gimlet would clear it out," said Char-ley Marden, " if we only had one."

THE STORY OF A BAD BOY

Cleaning Her Out

I looked to see if Sailor Ben's flag was flying atthe cabin door, for he always took in the colorswhen he went off fishing.

" When you want to know if the Admiral'saboard, jest cast an eye to the bun tin', my heart-ies," says Sailor Ben.

Sometimes in a jocose mood he called himselfthe Admiral, and I am sure he deserved to be one.The Admiral's flag was flying, and I soon pro-cured a gimlet from his carefully kept tool-chest.

Before long we had the gun in working order.A newspaper lashed to the end of a lath served asa swab to dust out the bore. Jack Harris blewthrough the touch-hole and pronounced all clear.

Seeing our task accomplished so easily, weturned our attention to the other guns, which layin all sorts of postures in the rank grass. Bor-rowing a rope from Sailor Ben, we managed withimmense labor to drag the heavy pieces into posi-tion and place a brick under each muzzle to give itthe proper elevation. When we beheld them allin a row, like a regular battery, we simultaneouslyconceived an idea, the magnitude of which struckus dumb for a moment.

Our first intention was to load and fire a singlegun. How feeble and insignificant was such aplan compared to that which now sent the lightdancing into our eyes !

"What could we have been thinking of?"cried Jack Harris. " We '11 give 'em a broadside,to be sure, if we die for it!'

We turned to with a will, and before nightfallhad nearly half the battery overhauled and readyfor service. To keep the artillery dry we stuffedwads of loose hemp into the muzzles, and fittedwooden pegs to the touch-holes.

At recess the next noon the Centipedes met ina corner of the school-yard to talk over the pro-posed lark. The original projectors, though theywould have liked to keep the thing secret, wereobliged to make a club matter of it, inasmuch asfunds were required for ammunition. There hadbeen no recent drain on the treasury, and the so-ciety could well afford to spend a few dollars in sonotable an undertaking.

It was unanimously agreed that the plan shouldbe carried out in the handsomest manner, and asubscription to that end was taken on the spot.Several of the Centipedes had n't a cent, exceptingthe one strung around their necks ; others, how-ever, were richer. I chanced to have a dollar,and it went into the cap quicker than lightning.When the club, in view of my munificence, votedto name the guns Bailey's Battery, I was prouderthan I have ever been since over anything.

The money thus raised, added to that already inthe treasury, amounted to nine dollars — a for-tune in those days; but not more than we had usefor. This sum was divided into twelve parts, forit would not do for one boy to buy all the powder,nor even for us all to make our purchases at thesame place. That would excite suspicion at anytime, particularly at a period so remote from theFourth of July.

There were only three stores in town licensedto sell powder; that gave each store four custom-ers. Not to run the slightest risk of remark,one boy bought his powder on Monday, the nextboy on Tuesday, and so on until the requisitequantity was in our possession. This we put intoa keg and carefully hid in a dry spot on the wharf.

Our next step was to finish cleaning the guns,which occupied two afternoons, for several ofthe old sogers were in a very congested state in-deed. Having completed the task, we came upon

a difficulty. To set off the battery by daylightwas out of the question; it must be done at night;it must be done with fuses, for no doubt theneighbors would turn out after the first two orthree shots, and it would not pay to be caught inthe vicinity.

Who knew anything about fuses ? Who couldarrange it so the guns would go off one after theother, with an interval of a minute or so between ?

Theoretically we knew that a minute fuse lasteda minute ; double the quantity, two minutes ; butpractically we were at a stand-still. There wasbut one person who could help us in this extrem-ity— Sailor Ben. To me was assigned the dutyof obtaining what information I could from theex-gunner, it being left to my discretion whetheror not to irutrtist him with our secret.

So one evening I dropped into the cabin andartfully turned the conversation to fuses in gen-eral, and then to particular fuses, but withoutgetting much out of the old boy, who was busymaking a twine hammock. Finally, I was forcedto divulge the whole plot.

The Admiral had a sailor's love for a joke, andentered at once and heartily into our scheme.He volunteered to prepare the fuses himself, andI left the labor in his hands, having bound himby several extraordinary oaths — such as " Hope-I-may-die " and " May I sink first " — not to be-tray us, come what would.

This was Monday evening. On Wednesdaythe fuses were ready. That night we were to un-muzzle Bailey's Battery. Mr. Grimshaw saw thatsomething was wrong somewhere, for we wererestless and absent-minded in the classes, and thebest of us came to grief before the morning ses-sion was over. When Mr. Grimshaw announced"Guy Fawkes " as the subject for our next com-position, you might have knocked down the Mys-tic Twelve with a feather.

The coincidence was certainly curious, butwhen a man has committed, or is about to com-mit, an offense, a hundred trifles, which wouldpass unnoticed at another time, seem to point athim with convicting fingers. No doubt GuyFawkes himself received many a start after he hadgot his wicked kegs of gunpowder neatly piledup under the House of Lords.

Wednesday, as I have mentioned, was a half-holiday, and the Centipedes assembled in my barnto decide on the final arrangements. These wereas simple as could be. As the fuses were connected, it needed but one person to fire the train.Hereupon arose a discussion as to who was theproper person. Some argued that I ought toapply the match, the battery being christenedafter me, and the main idea, moreover, beingmine. Others advocated the claim of Phil Adamsas the oldest boy. At last we drew lots for thepost of honor.

Twelve slips of folded paper, upon one of whichwas written " Thou art the man," were placed ina quart measure, and thoroughly shaken ; theneach member stepped up and lifted out his des-tiny. At a given signal we opened our billets." Thou art the man," said the slip of paper trembling in my fingers. The sweets and anxieties ofa leader were mine the rest of the afternoon.

Directly after twilight set in, Phil Adams stoledown to the wharf and fixed the fuses to the guns,laying a train of powder from the principal fuse tothe fence, through a chink of which I was to dropthe match at midnight.

At ten o'clock Rivermouth goes to bed. Ateleven o'clock Rivermouth is as quiet as a country churchyard. At twelve o'clock there is no-thing left with which to compare the stillness thatbroods over the little seaport.

In the midst of this stillness I arose and glidedout of the house like a phantom bent on an evilerrand ; like a phantom I flitted through the si-lent street, hardly drawing breath until I kneltdown beside the fence at the appointed place.

Pausing a moment for my heart to stop thump-ing, I lighted the match and shielded it with bothhands until it was well under way, and thendropped the blazing splinter on the slender threadof gunpowder.

A noiseless flash instantly followed, and allwas dark again. I peeped through the crevice in

the fence, and saw the main fuse spitting outsparks like a conjurer. Assured that the trainhad not failed, I took to my heels, fearful lest thefuse might burn more rapidly than we calculated,and cause an explosion before I could get home.This, luckily, did not happen. There is a spe-cial Providence that watches over idiots, drunkenmen, and boys.

I dodged the ceremony of undressing by plung-ing into bed, jacket, boots, and all. I am notsure I took off my cap ; but I know that I hadhardly pulled the coverlid over me, when " BOOM !"sounded the first gun of Bailey's Battery.

I lay as still as a mouse. In less than two min-utes there was another burst of thunder, and thenanother. The third gun was a tremendous fellowand fairly shook the house.

The town was waking up. Windows werethrown open here and there, and people calledto each other across the streets asking what thatfiring was for.

" BOOM !' went gun number four.

I sprung out of bed and tore off my jacket, forI heard the Captain feeling his way along thewall to my chamber. I was half undressed by thetime he found the knob of the door.

" I say, sir," I cried, " do you hear those guns!"

" Not being deaf, I do," said the Captain, alittle tartly — any reflection on his hearing alwaysnettled him; " but what on earth they are for I

 can't conceive. You had better get up and dress yourself."

" I 'm nearly dressed, sir."

" BOOM ! BOOM ! "—two of the guns had gone off together.

The door of Miss Ab-igail's bedroom opened hastily, and that pink of maidenly propriety stepped out into the hall in her night-gown— the only indecorous thing I ever knew her to do. She held a light-ed candle in her hand and looked like a very aged Lady Macbeth.

" O Dan'el, this is dreadful! What do you suppose it means ?'

"I really can't suppose," said the Captain, rub-bing his ear ; " but I guess it's over now."

" BOOM ! " said Bailey's Battery.

Rivermouth was wide awake now, and half the male population were in the streets, running dif-ferent ways, for the firing seemed to proceed from opposite points of the town. Everybody waylaid I everybody else with questions; but as no one knew what was the occasion of the tumult, people who were not usually nervous began to be op-pressed by the mystery.

Miss A bigail awakes

Some thought the town was being bombarded; some thought the world was coming to an end, as the pious and ingenious Mr. Miller had recently predicted it would ; but those who could not form any theory whatever were the most perplexed.

In the mean while Bailey's Battery bellowed

Bailey1's Battery booming away at regular intervals. The greatest confusionreigned everywhere by this time. People withlanterns rushed hither and thither. The town-watch had turned out to a man, and marched off, in admirable order, in the wrong direction. Dis-covering their mistake, they retraced their steps,and got down to the wharf just as the last cannonbelched forth its lightning.

A dense cloud of sulphurous smoke floated overAnchor Lane, obscuring the starlight. Two orthree hundred persons, in various stages of excite-ment, crowded about the upper end of the wharf,not liking to advance farther until they were satis-fied that the explosions were over. A board washere and there blown from the fence, and throughthe openings thus afforded a few of the more dar-ing spirits at last ventured to crawl.

The cause of the racket soon transpired. Asuspicion that they had been sold graduallydawned on the Rivermouthians. Many were ex-ceedingly indignant, and declared that no penaltywas severe enough for those concerned in sucha prank; others — and these were the very per-sons who had been terrified nearly out of theirwits—had the assurance to laugh, saying thatthey knew all along it was only a trick.

The town-watch boldly took possession of theground, and the crowd began to disperse. Knotsof gossips lingered here and there near the place,indulging in vain surmises as to who the invisiblegunners could be.

There was no more noise that night, but many atimid person lay awake expecting a renewal of themysterious cannonading. The Oldest Inhabitant refused to go to bed on any terms, but persistedin sitting up in a rocking-chair, with his hat andmittens on, until daybreak.

I thought I should never get to sleep. Themoment I drifted off in a doze I fell to laughingand woke myself up. But towards morning slum-ber overtook me, and I had a series of disagree-able dreams, in one of which I was waited uponby the ghost of Silas Trefethen with an exorbi-tant bill for the use of his guns. In another, Iwas dragged before a court-martial and sentencedby Sailor Ben, in a frizzled wig and three-corneredcocked hat, to be shot to death by Bailey's Bat-tery— a sentence which Sailor Ben was about toexecute with his own hand, when I suddenlyopened my eyes and found the sunshine lyingpleasantly across my face. I tell you I was glad!

That unaccountable fascination which leads theguilty to hover about the spot where his crimewas committed drew me down to the wharf assoon as I was dressed. Phil Adams, Jack Harris,and others of the conspirators were already there,examining with a mingled feeling of curiosity andapprehension the havoc accomplished by the bat*tery.

The fence was badly shattered and the groundploughed up for several yards round the placewhere the guns formerly lay — formerly lay, fornow they were scattered every which way. Therewas scarcely a gun that had not burst. Here was

one ripped open from muzzle to breech, and therewas another with its mouth blown into the shapeof a trumpet. Three of the guns had disappearedbodily, but on looking over the edge of the wharfwe saw them standing on end in the tide-mud.They had popped overboard in their excitement.

" I tell you what, fellows," whispered Phil Ad-ams, " it is lucky we did n't try to touch 'em offwith punk. They 'd have blown us all to flin-ders."

The destruction of Bailey's Battery was not,unfortunately, the only catastrophe. A fragmentof one of the cannon had carried away the chim-ney of Sailor Ben's cabin. He was very mad atfirst, but having prepared the fuse himself he didnot dare complain openly.

" I 'd have taken a reef in the blessed stove-pipe," said the Admiral, gazing ruefully at thesmashed chimney, "if I had known as how theFlagship was agoin* to be under fire."

The next day he rigged out an iron funnel,which, being in sections, could be detached andtaken in at a moment's notice. On the whole, Ithink he was resigned to the demolition of hisbrick chimney. The stove-pipe was a great dealmore ship-shape.

The town was not so easily appeased. Theselectmen determined to make an example of theguilty parties, and offered a reward for their ar-rest, holding out a promise of pardon to any one

of the offenders who would furnish informationagainst the rest. But there were no faint heartsamong the Centipedes. Suspicion rested for awhile on several persons — on the soldiers at thefort; on a crazy fellow, known about town as" Bottle-Nose ;' and at last on Sailor Ben.

" Shiver my timbers !' cries that deeply injuredindividual. " Do you suppose, sir, as I have livedto sixty year, an' ain't got no more sense thanto go for to blaze away at my own upper riggin' ?It does n't stand to reason."

It certainly did not seem probable that Mr.Watson would maliciously knock over his ownchimney, and Lawyer Hackett, who had the casein hand, bowed himself out of the Admiral's cabin,convinced that the right man had not been dis-covered.

People living by the sea are always more or lesssuperstitious. Stories of spectre ships and mys-terious beacons, that lure vessels out of theircourse and wreck them on unknown reefs, wereamong the stock legends of Rivermouth ; and nota few persons in the town were ready to attributethe firing of those guns to some supernaturalagency. The Oldest Inhabitant remembered thatwhen he was a boy a dim - looking sort ofschooner hove to in the offing one foggy after-noon, fired off a single gun that did not make anyreport, and then crumbled to nothing, spar, mast,and hulk, like a piece of burnt paper.

The authorities, however, were of the opinionthat human hands had something to do with theexplosions, and they resorted to deep-laid strata-gems to get hold of the said hands. One of theirtraps came very near catching us. They artfullycaused an old brass fieldpiece to be left on awharf near the scene of our late operations. No-thing in the world but the lack of money to buypowder saved us from falling into the clutches ofthe two watchmen who lay secreted for a week ina neighboring sail-loft.

It was many a day before the midnight bom-bardment ceased to be the town-talk. The trickwas so audacious and on so grand a scale thatnobody thought for an instant of connecting uslads with it. Suspicion at last grew weary oflighting on the wrong person, and as conjecture— like the physicians in the epitaph — was invain, the Rivermouthians gave up the idea of find-ing out who had astonished them.

They never did find out, and never will, unlessthey read this veracious history. If the selectmenare still disposed to punish the malefactors, I cansupply Lawyer Hackett with evidence enough toconvict Pepper Whitcomb, Phil Adams, CharleyHarden, and the other honorable members of theCentipede Club. But really I do not think it wouldpay now.

CHAPTER XVIII

A FROG HE WOULD A-WOOING GO

IF the reader supposes that I lived all thiswhile in Rivermouth without falling a victim toone or more of the young ladies attending MissDorothy Gibbs's Female Institute, why, then, allI have to say is the reader exhibits his ignoranceof human nature.

Miss Gibbs's seminary was located within a fewminutes' walk of the Temple Grammar School,and numbered about thirty-five pupils, the major-ity of whom boarded at the Hall— Primrose Hall,as Miss Dorothy prettily called it. The Prim-roses, as we called them, ranged from seven yearsof age to sweet seventeen, and a prettier group ofsirens never got together even in Rivermouth,for Rivermouth, you should know, is famous for itspretty girls.

There were tall girls and short girls, rosy girlsand pale girls, and girls as brown as berries ; girlslike Amazons, slender girls, weird and winninglike Undine, girls with black tresses, girls withauburn ringlets, girls with every tinge of goldenhair. To behold Miss Dorothy's young ladies ofa Sunday morning walking to church two by two,

the smallest toddling at the end of the procession,like the bobs at the tail of a kite, was a spectacleto fill with tender emotion the least susceptibleheart. To see Miss Dorothy marching grimly atthe head of her light infantry, was to feel thehopelessness of making an attack on any part ofthe column.

She was a perfect dragon of watchfulness. Themost unguarded lifting of an eyelash in the flut-tering battalion was sufficient to put her on thelookout. She had had experiences with the malesex, this Miss Dorothy so prim and grim. It waswhispered that her heart was a tattered albumscrawled over with love-lines, but that she hadshut up the volume long ago.

There was a tradition that she had been crossedin love ; but it was the faintest of traditions. Agay young lieutenant of marines had flirted withher at a country ball (A. D. 1811), and thenmarched carelessly away at the head of his com-pany to the shrill music of the fife, without somuch as a sigh for the girl he left behind him.The years rolled on, the gallant gay Lothario —which was not his name — married, became a fa-ther, and then a grandfather; and at the period ofwhich I am speaking his grandchild was actuallyone of Miss Dorothy's young ladies. So, at least,ran the story.

The lieutenant himself was dead these manyyears ; but Miss Dorothy never got over his du-

plicity. She was convinced that the sole aim ofmankind was to win the unguarded affection ofmaidens, and then march off treacherously withflying colors to the heartless music of the drumand fife. To shield the inmates of Primrose Hallfrom the bitter influences that had blighted herown early affections was Miss Dorothy's missionin life.

" No wolves prowling about my lambs, if youplease," said Miss Dorothy. " I will not allow it."

She was as good as her word. I do not thinkthe boy lives who ever set foot within the limitsof Primrose Hall while the seminary was underher charge. Perhaps if Miss Dorothy had givenher young ladies a little more liberty, they wouldnot have thought it " such fun ' to make eyesover the white lattice fence at the young gen-tlemen of the Temple Grammar School. I sayperhaps ; for it is one thing to manage thirty-five young ladies and quite another thing to talkabout it.

But all Miss Dorothy's vigilance could not pre-vent the young folks from meeting in the townnow and then, nor could her utmost ingenuity in-terrupt postal arrangements. There was no endof notes passing between the students and thePrimroses. Notes tied to the heads of arrowswere shot into dormitory windows ; notes weretucked under fences, and hidden in the trunks ofdecayed trees. Every thick place in the boxwood

231

hedge that surrounded the seminary was a possi-ble post-office.

It was a terrible shock to Miss Dorothy the dayshe unearthed a nest of letters in one of the hugewooden urnssurmounting thegateway that ledto her dovecot.It was a bittermoment to MissPhoebe and MissCandace andMiss Hesba,when they hadtheir locks ofhair grimlyhanded back tothem by MissGibbs in thepresence of thewhole school.Girls whoselocks of hair had run the blockade in safety wereparticularly severe on the offenders. But it didnot stop other notes and other tresses, and Iwould like to know what can stop them while theearth holds together.

Now when I first came to Rivermouth I lookedupon girls as rather tame company; I had not aspark of sentiment concerning them; but seeing

The Discovery

my comrades sending and receiving mysteriousepistles, wearing bits of ribbon in their button-holes, and leaving packages of confectionery (gen-erally lemon-drops) in the hollow trunks of trees— why, I felt that this was the proper thing todo. I resolved, as a matter of duty, to fall in lovewith somebody, and I did not care in the leastwho it was. In much the same mood that DonQuixote selected the Dulcinea del

Toboso for his lady-love, I singled out one of Miss Dorothy's in-comparable young ladies for mine.

I debated a long while whether I should not select two, but at last settled down on one — a pale little girl with blue eyes, named Alice. I shall not make a long story of this, for Alice made short work of me. She was secretly in love with Pepper Whitcomb. This occasioned a temporary coolness between Pepper and myself.

Not disheartened, however, I placed Laura Rice — I believe it was Laura Rice — in the va-cant niche. The new idol was more cruel than the old. The former frankly sent me to the right about, but the latter was a deceitful lot. She wore my nosegay in her dress at the evening ser-vice (the Primroses were marched to church three times every Sunday), she penned me the daintiest of notes, she sent me the glossiest of ringlets (cut, as I afterwards found out, from the stupid head of Miss Gibbs's chambermaid), and at the same time was holding me and my pony up to ridicule in

a series of letters written to Jack Harris. It was Harris himself who kindly opened my eyes.

" I tell you what, Bailey," said that young gen-tleman, " Laura is an old veteran, and carries too many guns for a youngster. She can't resist a flirtation ; I believe she 'd flirt with an infant in arms. There 's hardly a fellow in the school that has n't worn her colors and some of her hair. She does n't give out any more of her own hair now. She had to stop that. The demand was greater than the supply, you see. It's all very well to correspond with Laura, but as to looking for anything serious from her, the knowing ones don't. Hope I have n't hurt your feelings, old boy " (that was a soothing stroke of flattery to call me "old boy"), "but 'twas my duty as a friend and a Centipede to let you know who you were dealing with."

Such was the advice given me by that time-stricken, careworn, and embittered man of the world, who was sixteen years old if he was a day.

I dropped Laura. In the course of the next twelve months I had perhaps three or four similar experiences, and the conclusion was forced upon me that I was not a boy likely to distinguish myself in this branch of business.

I fought shy of Primrose Hall from that mo-ment. Smiles were smiled over the boxwood hedge, and little hands were occasionally kissed to me; but I only winked my eye patronizingly, and

passed on. I never renewed tender relations with Miss Gibbs's young ladies. All this occurred dur-ing my first year and a half at Rivermouth.

Between my studies at school, my out-door recreations, and the hurts my vanity received, I managed to escape for the time being any very serious attack of that love fever which, like the measles, is almost certain to seize upon a boy sooner or later. I was not to be an exception. I was merely biding my time. The incidents I have now to relate took place shortly after the events described in the last chapter.

In a life so tranquil and circumscribed as ours in the Nutter House, a visitor was a novelty of no little importance. The whole household awoke from its quietude one morning when the Captain announced that a young niece of his from New York was to spend a few weeks with us.

The blue chintz room, into which a ray of sun was never allowed to penetrate, was thrown open and dusted, and its mouldy air made sweet with a bouquet of pot-roses placed on the old-fashioned bureau. Kitty was busy all the forenoon washing off the sidewalk and sand-papering the great brass knocker on our front door ; and Miss Abigail was up to her elbows in a pigeon-pie.

I felt sure it was for no ordinary person that all these preparations were in progress; and I was right. Miss Nelly Glentworth was no ordinary

person. I shall never believe she was. There may have been lovelier women, though I havenever seen them; there may have been morebrilliant women, though it has not been my fortuneto meet them; but that there was ever a morecharming one than Nelly Glentworth is a propo-sition against which I contend.

I do not love her now. I do not think of heronce in five years; and yet it would give me aturn if in the course of my daily walk I shouldsuddenly come upon her eldest boy. I may saythat her eldest boy was not playing a prominentpart in this life when I first made her acquaint-ance.

It was a drizzling, cheerless afternoon towardsthe end of summer that a hack drew up at thedoor of the Nutter House. The Captain and MissAbigail hastened into the hall on hearing thecarriage stop. In a moment more Miss NellyGlentworth was seated in our sitting-room under-going a critical examination at the hands of asmall boy who lounged uncomfortably on a setteebetween the windows.

The small boy considered himself a judge ofgirls, and he rapidly came to the following conclu-sions : That Miss Nellie was about nineteen ; thatshe had not given away much of her back hair,which hung in two massive chestnut braids overher shoulders ; that she was a shade too pale anda trifle too tall; that her hands were nicely

shaped and her feet much too diminutive for dailyuse. He furthermore observed that her voice wasmusical, and that her face lighted up with an in-describable brightness when she smiled.

On the whole, the small boy liked her wellenough; and, satisfied that she was not a personto be afraid of, but, on the contrary, one whomight turn out to be quite agreeable, he departedto keep an appointment with his friend Sir PepperWhitcomb.

But the next morning, when Miss Glentworthcame down to breakfast in a purple dress, her faceas fresh as one of the moss-roses on the bureauupstairs, and her laugh as contagious as the mer-riment of a robin, the small boy experienced astrange sensation, and mentally compared herwith the loveliest of Miss Gibbs's young ladies, andfound those young ladies wanting in the balance.

A night's rest had wrought a wonderful changejn Miss Nelly. The pallor and weariness of thejourney had passed away. I looked at her throughthe toast rack and thought I had never seen any-thing more winning than her smile.

After breakfast she went out with me to thestable to see Gypsy, and the three of us becamefriends then and there. Nelly was the only girlthat Gypsy ever took the slightest notice of.

It chanced to be a half-holiday, and a base-ballmatch of unusual interest was to come off on theschool ground that afternoon; but, somehow, I

did not go. I hung about the house abstractedly.The Captain went up town, and Miss Abigail wasbusy in the kitchen making immortal gingerbread.I drifted into the sitting-room, and had our guestall to myself for I do not know how many hours.It was twilight, I recollect, when the Captainreturned with letters for Miss Nelly.

Many a time after that I sat with her throughthe dreamy September afternoons. If I hadplayed base-ball it would have been much betterfor me.

Those first days of Miss Nelly's visit are verymisty in my remembrance. I try in vain to re-member just when I began to fall in love with her.Whether the spell worked upon me gradually orfell upon me all at once, I do not know. I onlyknow that it seemed to me as if I had alwaysloved her. Things that took place before shecame were dim to me, like events that had oc-curred in the Middle Ages.

Nelly was at least five years my senior. Butwhat of that ? Adam is the only man I everheard of who did not in early youth fall in lovewith a woman older than himself, and I am con-vinced that he would have done so if he had hadthe opportunity.

I wonder if girls from fifteen to twenty areaware of the glamour they cast over the stragglingawkward boys whom they regard and treat as merechildren. I wonder, now. Young women are so

keen in such matters. I wonder if Miss NellyGlentworth never suspected until the very lastnight of her visit at Rivermouth that I was overears in love with her pretty self, and was sufferingpangs as poignant as if I had been ten feet highand as old as Methuselah. For, indeed, I wasmiserable throughout all those five weeks. I wentdown in the Latin class at the rate of three boysa day. Her fresh young eyes came between meand my book, and there was an end of Virgil

" O love, love, love I

Love is like a dizziness,It winna let a body

Gang about his business."

I was wretched away from her, and only lesswretched in her presence. The especial cause ofmy woe was this : I was simply a little boy to MissGlentworth. I knew it. I bewailed it. I groundmy teeth and wept in secret over the fact. If Ihad bcen aught else in her eyes would she havesmoothed my hair so carelessly, sending an elec-tric shock through my whole system ? would shehave walked with me, hand in hand, for hours inthe old garden ? and once when I lay on thesofa, my head aching with love and mortification,would she have stooped down and kissed me if Ihad not been a little boy. How I despised littleboys ! How I hated one particular little boy — toolittle to be loved !

I smile over this very grimly even now. My

sorrow was genuine and bitter. It is a great mis-take on the part of elderly ladies, male and female,to tell a child that he is seeing his happiest days.Do not you believe a word of it, my little friend.The burdens of childhood are as hard to bear asthe crosses that weigh us down later in life, whilethe happinesses of childhood are tame comparedwith those of our maturer years. And even ifthis were not so, it is rank cruelty to throwshadows over the young heart by croaking, "Bemerry, for to-morrow you die !'

As the last days of Nellie's visit drew near, Ifell into a very unhealthy state of mind. To haveher so frank and unconsciously coquettish withme was a daily torment; to be looked upon andtreated as a child was bitter almonds; but thethought of losing her altogether was distraction.

The summer was at an end. The days wereperceptibly shorter, and now and then came anevening when it was chilly enough to have a woodfire in our sitting-room. The leaves were begin-ning to take hectic tints, and the wind was prac-ticing the minor pathetic notes of its autumnaldirge. Nature and myself appeared to be ap-proaching our dissolution simultaneously.

One evening, the evening previous to the dayset for Nelly's departure — how well I rememberit! — I found her sitting alone by the wide chim-ney-piece looking musingly at the crackling back-There were no candles in the room. On

The Last Evening

her face and hands, and on the small golden cross at her throat, fell the flickering firelight -— that ruddy, mellow firelight in which one's grandmo-ther would look poetical.

I drew a low stool from the corner and placed it by the side of her chair. She reached out her hand to me, as was her pretty fashion, and so we sat for several moments silently in the changing

glow of the burning logs. Presently I moved back the stool so that I could see her face in profile without being seen by her. I lost her hand by this movement, but I could not have spoken with the listless touch of her fingers on mine. After two or three attempts I said " Nelly " a good deal louder than I intended.

Perhaps the effort it cost me was evident in my voice. She raised herself quickly in the chair and half turned towards me.

 Well, Tom ?"

"I — I am very sorry you are going away."

" So am I. I have enjoyed every hour of my visit."

" Do you think you will ever come back here ?"

" Perhaps," said Nelly, and her eyes wandered off into the fitful firelight.

" I suppose you will forget us all very quickly."

" Indeed I shall not. I shall always have the pleasantest recollections of Rivermouth."

Here the conversation died a natural death. Nelly sank into a sort of dream, and I meditated. Fearing every moment to be interrupted by some member of the family, I nerved myself to make a bold dash.

"Nelly."

"Well."

" Do you " — I hesitated.

" Do I what ?"

" Love any one very much ? "

" Why, of course I do," said Nelly, scatteringher revery with a merry laugh. "I love UncleNutter and Aunt Nutter, and you — and Towser."

Towser, our new dog! I could not stand thatI pushed back the stool impatiently and stood infront of her.

" That's not what I mean," I said angrily.

" Well, what do you mean ?"

" Do you love any one to marry him ?"

" The idea of it," cried Nelly, laughing.

" But you must tell me."

" Must, Tom ?"

" Indeed you must, Nelly."

She had risen from the chair with an amused,perplexed look in her eyes. I held her an instantby the dress.

" Please tell me."

" Oh you silly boy !" cried Nelly. Then sherumpled my hair all over my forehead and ranlaughing out of the room.

Suppose Cinderella had rumpled the prince'shair all over his forehead, how would he have likedit? Suppose the Sleeping Beauty when theking's son with a kiss set her and all the oldclocks agoing in the spellbound castle — supposethe young minx had looked up and coolly laughedin his eye, I guess the king's son would not havebeen greatly pleased.

I hesitated a second or two and then rushedafter Nelly just in time to run against Miss gail, who entered the room with a couple of lightedcandles.

" Goodness gracious, Tom !' exclaimed MissAbigail, " are you possessed ?'

I left her scraping the warm spermaceti fromone of her thumbs.

Nelly was in the kitchen talking quite uncon-cernedly with Kitty Collins. There she remaineduntil supper-time. Supper over, we all adjournedto the sitting-room. Iplanned and plotted,but could manage in noway to get Nelly alone.She and the Captainplayed cribbage all theevening.

The next morning •«,my lady did not make * |her appearance untilwe were seated at thebreakfast-table. I hadgot up at daylight my-self. Immediately afterbreakfast the carriagearrived to take her to

Removing the Spermaceti

the railway station. A

gentleman stepped from this carriage, and greatlyto my surprise was warmly welcomed by the Cap-tain and Miss Abigail, and by Miss Nelly herself,who seemed unnecessarily glad to see him. From

the hasty conversation that followed I learned thatthe gentleman had come somewhat unexpectedlyto conduct Miss Nelly to Boston. But how didhe know that she was to leave that morning?Nelly bade farewell to the Captain and MissAbigail, made a little rush and kissed me on thenose, and was gone.

As the wheels of the hack rolled up the streetand over my finer feelings, I turned to the Cap-tain.

" Who was that gentleman, sir ?"

"That was Mr. Waldron."

" A relation of yours, sir ?" I asked craftily.

" No relation of mine — a relation of Nelly's/'said the Captain, smiling.

"A cousin," I suggested, feeling a strange ha-tred spring up in my bosom for the unknown.

" Well, I suppose you might call him a cousinfor the present. He 's going to marry little Nellynext summer."

In one of Peter Parley's valuable historicalworks is a description of an earthquake at Lisbon."At the first shock the inhabitants rushed intothe streets; the earth yawned at their feet and thehouses tottered and fell on every side." I stag-gered past the Captain into the street; a giddi-ness came over me; the earth yawned at my feet,and the houses threatened to fall in on every sideof me. How distinctly I remember that momen-tary sense of confusion when everything in theworld seemed toppling over into ruins.

As I have remarked, my love for Nelly is a thingof the past. I had not thought of her for yearsuntil I sat down to write this chapter, and yet, nowthat all is said and done, I should not care particu-larly to come across Mrs. Waldron's eldest boy inmy afternoon's walk. He must be fourteen or fif-teen years old by this time — the young villain 1

CHAPTER XIX

I BECOME A BLIGHTED BEING

WHEN a young boy gets to be an old boy, whenthe hair is growing rather thin on the top ofthe old boy's head, and he has been tamed suffi-ciently to take a sort of chastened pleasure inallowing the baby to play with his watch-seals —when, I say, an old boy has reached this stage inthe journey of life, he is sometimes apt to indulgein sportive remarks concerning his first love.

Now, though I bless my stars that it was not in my power to marry Miss Nelly, I am not going to deny my boyish regard for her nor laugh at it. As long as it lasted it was a very sincere and unselfish love, and rendered me proportionately wretched. I say as long as it lasted, for one's first love does not last forever.

I am ready, however, to laugh at the amusing figure I cut after I had really ceased to have any deep feeling in the matter. It was then I took it into my head to be a Blighted Being. This was about two weeks after the spectral appearance of Mr. Waldron.

For a boy of a naturally vivacious disposition, the part of a blighted being presented difficulties.

247

In Love

I had an excellent appetite, I liked society, I liked out-of-door sports, I was fond of handsome clothes. Now all these things were incompatible. with the doleful character I was to assume, and I proceeded to cast them from me. I neglected my hair. I avoided my play-mates. I frowned ab-stractedly. I did not eat as much as was good for me. I took lonely walks. I brood-ed in solitude. I not only committed to memory the more tur-gid poems of the late Lord Byron — "Fare thee well, and if forever," etc. — but I became a de-spondent poet on my own account, and composed a string of " Stanzas to One who will understand them." I think I was a trifle too hopeful on that point; for I came across the verses several years afterwards, and was quite unable to understand them myself.

It was a great comfort to be so perfectly miser-able and yet not surfer any. I used to look in the glass and gloat over the amount and variety of mournful expressions I could throw into my fea-tures. If I caught myself smiling at anything, I cut the smile short with a sigh. The oddest thing about all this is, I never once suspected that I

248 THE STORY OF A BAD BOY

was not unhappy. No one, not even Pepper Whit-comb, was more deceived than I.

Among the minor pleasures of being blighted were the interest and perplexity I excited in the simple souls that were thrown in daily contact with me. Pepper especially. I nearly drove him into a corresponding state of mind.

I had from time to time given Pepper slight but impressive hints of my admiration for Some One (this was in the early part of Miss Glentworth's visit) ; I had also led him to infer that my admira-tion was not altogether in vain. He was therefore unable to explain the cause of my strange behavior, for I had carefully refrained from mentioning to Pepper the fact that Some One had turned out to be Another's.

I treated Pepper shabbily. I could not resist playing on his tenderer feelings. He was a boy bubbling over with sympathy for any one in any kind of trouble. Our intimacy since Binny Wal-lace's death had been uninterrupted; but now I moved in a sphere apart, not to be profaned by the step of an outsider.

I no longer joined the boys on the playgroundat recess. I stayed at my desk reading some lu-gubrious volume — usually The Mysteries of Udol-pho, by the amiable Mrs. Radcliffe. A translationof The Sorrows of Werther fell into my hands atthis period, and if I could have committed suicidewithout killing myself, I should certainly havedone so.

On half-holidays, instead of fraternizing withPepper and the rest of our clique, I would wanderoff alone to Grave Point.

Grave Point — the place where Binny Wallace'sbody came ashore — was a narrow strip of landrunning out into the river. A line of Lombardypoplars, stiff and severe, like a row of grenadiers,mounted guard on the water-side. On the ex-treme end of the peninsula was an old disusedgraveyard, tenanted principally by the early set-tlers who had been scalped by the Indians. In aremote corner of the cemetery, set apart from theother mounds, was the grave of a woman who hadbeen hanged in the old colonial times for themurder of her infant. Goodwife Polly Haines haddenied the crime to the last, and after her deaththere had arisen strong doubts as to her actualguilt. It was a belief current among the lads ofthe town, that if you went to this grave at night-fall on the loth of November—the anniversaryof her execution —and asked, "For what did themagistrates hang you?" a voice would reply," Nothing."

Many a Rivermouth boy has tremblingly putthis question in the dark, and, sure enough, PollyHaines invariably answered nothing!

A low red-brick wall, broken down in manyplaces and frosted over with silvery moss, sur-rounded this burial-ground of our Pilgrim Fathersand their immediate descendants. The latest date

on any of the headstones was 1760. A crop ofvery funny epitaphs sprung up here and thereamong the overgrown thistles and burdocks, andalmost every tablet had a death's-head with cross-bones engraved upon it, or else a puffy round facewith a pair of wings stretching out from the ears,like this:

These mortuary emblems furnished me withcongenial food for reflection. I used to lie in thelong grass, and speculate on the advantages anddisadvantages of being a cherub.

I forget what I thought the advantages were,but I remember distinctly of getting into an inex-tricable tangle on two points : How could a cherub,being all head and wings, manage to sit downwhen he was tired ? To have to sit down on theback of his head struck me as an awkward alter-native. Again: Where did a cherub carry thoseindispensable articles (such as jackknives, marbles,and pieces of twine) which boys in an earthly stateof existence usually stow away in their trouserspockets ?

These were knotty questions, and I was neverable to dispose of them satisfactorily.

I am a Blighted Being

Meanwhile Pepper Whitcomb would scour the whole town in search of me. He finally discov-ered my retreat, and dropped in on me abruptly one afternoon, while I was deep in the cherub problem.

" Look here, Tom Bailey!" said Pepper, shying a piece of clam-shell indignantly at the Hic jacet on a neighboring gravestone, "you are just going to the dogs ! Can't you tell a fellow what in thun-der ails you, instead of prowling round among the tombs like a jolly old vampire ?'

" Pepper," I replied, solemnly, " don't ask me ; you would n't understand. Some day you may. You are too fat and thoughtless now."

Pepper stared at me.

"Earthly happiness," I continued, "is a delu-sion and a snare. You will never be happy, Pep-per, until you are a cherub."

Pepper, by the by, would have made an excel-lent cherub, he was so chubby. Having delivered myself of these gloomy remarks, I arose languidly from the grass and moved away, leaving Pepper staring after me in mute astonishment. I was Hamlet and Werther and the late Lord

Byron all in one.

You will ask what my purpose was in cultivat-ing this factitious despondency. None whatever. Blighted Beings never have any purpose in life excepting to be as blighted as possible.

Of course my present line of business could not long escape the eye of Captain Nutter. I do not know if the Captain suspected my attachment for Miss Glentworth. He never alluded to it; but he watched me. Miss Abigail watched me, Kitty Collins watched me, and Sailor Ben watched me.

" I can't make out his signals," I overheard the Admiral remark to my grandfather one day. "I, hope he ain't got no kind of sickness aboard."

There was something singularly agreeable in being an object of so great interest. Sometimes I had all I could do to preserve my dejected as-pect, it was so pleasant to be miserable. I incline to the opinion that persons who are melancholy without any particular reason, such as poets, ar-tists, and young musicians with long hair, have rather an enviable time of it. In a quiet way I never enjoyed myself better in my life than when I was a Blighted Being.

CHAPTER XX

IN WHICH I PROVE MYSELF TO BE THE GRANDSON OF MY GRANDFATHER

IT was not possible for a boy of my temper-ament to be a blighted being longer than three consecutive weeks.

I was gradually emerging from my self-imposed cloud when events took place that greatly assisted in restoring me to a more natural frame of mind. I awoke from an imaginary trouble to face a real one.

I suppose you do not know what a financial crisis is ? I will give you an illustration.

You are deeply in debt — say to the amount of a quarter of a dollar— to the little knicknack shop round the corner, where they sell picture-papers, spruce-gum, needles, and Malaga raisins. A boy owes you a quarter of a dollar, which he promises to pay at a certain time. You are depending on this quarter to settle accounts with the small shopkeeper. The time arrives — and the quarter does not. That 's a financial crisis, in one sense— in twenty-five senses, if I may say so.

When this same thing happens, on a grander scale, in the mercantile world, it produces what is called a panic. One man's inability to pay his debts ruins another man, who, in turn, ruins someone else, and so on, until failure after failure makes even the richest capitalists tremble. Pub-lic confidence is suspended, and the smaller fry of merchants are knocked over like tenpins.

These commercial panics occur periodically, after the fashion of comets and earthquakes and other disagreeable things. Such a panic took place in New Orleans in the year 18— and my fa-ther's banking-house went to pieces in the crash.

Of a comparatively large fortune nothing re-mained after paying his debts excepting a few thousand dollars, with which he proposed to re-turn North and embark in some less hazardous enterprise. In the mean time it was necessary for him to stay in New Orleans to wind up the business.

My grandfather was in some way involved in this failure, and lost, I fancy, a considerable sum of money; but he never talked much on the sub-ject. He was an unflinching believer in the spilt-milk proverb.

" It can't be gathered up," he would say, " and it's no use crying over it. Pitch into the cow and get some more milk, is my motto."

The suspension of the banking-house was bad enough, but there was an attending circumstance that gave us, at Rivermouth, a great deal more anxiety. The cholera, which some one predicted would visit the country that year, and which, in-deed, had made its appearance in a mild form atseveral points along the Mississippi River, hadbroken out with much violence at New Orleans.

The report that first reached us through thenewspapers was meagre and contradictory ; manypersons discredited it; but a letter from my motherleft us no room for doubt. The sickness was inthe city. The hospitals were filling up, and hun-dreds of the citizens were flying from the strickenplace by every steamboat. The unsettled state ofmy father's affairs made it imperative for him toremain at his post; his desertion at that momentwould have been at the sacrifice of all he hadsaved from the general wreck.

As he would be detained in New Orleans atleast three months, my mother declined to comeNorth without him.

After this we awaited with feverish impatiencethe weekly news that came to us from the South.The next letter advised us that my parentswere well, and that the sickness, so far, had notpenetrated to the faubourg, or district, wherethey lived. The following week brought lesscheering tidings. My father's business, in con-sequence of the flight of the other partners,'would keep him in the city beyond the period he^had mentioned. The family had moved to PassChristian, a favorite watering-place on LakePontchartrain, near New Orleans, where he was

able to spend part of each week. So the returnNorth was postponed indefinitely.

It was now that the old longing to see myparents came back to me with irresistible force.I knew my grandfather would not listen to theidea of my going to New Orleans at such a dan-gerous time, since he had opposed the journey sostrongly when the same objection did not exist.But I determined to go nevertheless.

I think I have mentioned the fact that all themale members of our family, on my father's side— as far back as the Middle Ages — have exhib-ited in early youth a decided talent for runningaway. It was an hereditary talent. It ran in theblood to run away. I do not pretend to explainthe peculiarity. I simply admit it.

It was not my fate to change the prescribedorder of things. I, too, was to run away, therebyproving, if any proof were needed, that I was thegrandson of my grandfather. I do not hold myselfresponsible for the step any more than I do forthe shape of my nose, which is said to be a fac-simile of Captain Nutter's.

I have frequently noticed how circumstancesconspire to help a man, or a boy, when he hasthoroughly resolved on doing a thing. That veryweek the Rivermouth Barnacle printed an adver-tisement that seemed to have been written onpurpose for me. It read as follows;

WANTED.— A Few ABLE-BODIED SEAMEN and a Cabin-Boy, forthe ship Rawlings, now loading for New Orleans at Johnson's Wharf,Boston. Apply in person, within four days, at the office of Messrs. & Co., or on board the Ship.

How I was to get to New Orleans with only$4.62 was a question that had been bothering me., This advertisement made it as clear as day. I.would go as cabin-boy.

I had taken Pepper into my confidence again;I had told him the story of my love for MissGlentworth, with all its harrowing details ; andnow conceived it judicious to confide in him thechange about to take place in my life, so that, ifthe Rawlings went down in a gale, my friendsmight have the limited satisfaction of knowingwhat had become of me.

Pepper shook his head discouragingly, andsought in every way to dissuade me from thestep. He drew a disenchanting picture of theexistence of a cabin-boy, whose constant duty(according to Pepper) was to have dishes brokenover his head whenever the captain or the matechanced to be out of humor, which was mostly allthe time. But nothing Pepper said could turnme a hair's breadth from my purpose.

I had little time to spare, for the advertisementstated explicitly that applications were to be madein person within four days. I trembled to thinkof the bare possibility of some other boy snappingup that desirable situation.

It was on Monday that I stumbled upon the

advertisement. On Tuesday my preparationswere completed. My baggage — consisting offour shirts, half a dozen collars, a piece of shoe-maker's wax (Heaven knows what for!), and fivestockings, wrapped in a silk handkerchief — layhidden under a loose plank of the stable floor.This was my point of departure.

My plan was to take the last train for Boston,in order to prevent the possibility of immediatepursuit, if any should be attempted. The trainleft at 4 p. M.

I ate no breakfast and little dinner that day. Iavoided the Captain's eye, and would not havelooked Miss Abigail or Kitty in the face for thewealth of the Indies.

When it was time to start for the station I re-tired quietly to the stable and uncovered my bun-dle. I lingered a moment to kiss the white staron Gypsy's forehead, and was nearly unmannedwhen the little animal returned the caress by lap-ping my cheek. Twice I went back and pattedher.

On reaching the station I purchased my ticketwith a bravado air that ought to have aroused thesuspicion of the ticket-master, and hurried to thecar, where I sat fidgeting until the train shot outinto the broad daylight.

Then I drew a long breath and looked aboutme. The first object that saluted my sight wasSailor Ben, four or five seats behind me, readingthe Rivermouth Barnacle!

Reading was not an easy art to Sailor Ben ; hegrappled with the sense of a paragraph as if itwere a polar bear, and generally got the worst ofit. On the present occasion he was having a hardstruggle, judging by the way he worked his mouthand rolled his eyes. He had evidently not seenme. But what was he doing on the Boston train ?

Without lingering to solve the question, I stolegently from my seat and passed into the forwardcar.

This was very awkward, having the Admiral onboard. I could not understand it at all. Could itbe possible that the old boy had got tired of landand was running away to sea himself? That wastoo absurd a supposition. I glanced nervously to-wards the car door now and then, half expectingto see him come after me.

We had passed one or two way-stations, and Ihad quieted down a good deal, when I began tofeel as if somebody was looking steadily at theback of my head. I turned round involuntarilyand there was Sailor Ben again, at the farther endof the car, wrestling with the Rivermouth Bar-nacle as before.

I began to grow very uncomfortable indeed.Was it by design or chance that he thus doggedmy steps ? If he was aware of my presence, whydid he not speak to me at once ? Why did hesteal round, making no sign, like a particularlyunpleasant phantom ? Maybe it was not Sailor

THE STORY OF A BAD BOY

Ben. I peeped at him slyly. There was no mis-taking that tanned, genial phiz of his. Very oddhe did not see me !

Literature, even in the mild form of a countrynewspaper, always had the effect of poppies onthe Admiral. When I stole another glance in hisdirection his hat was tilted over his right eye inthe most dissolute style, and the Rivermouth Bar-nacle lay in a con-fused heap besidehim. He had suc-cumbed. He wasfast asleep. If hewould only keepasleep until wereached our destina-tion

!

By and by I dis-covered that therear car had beendetached from the train at the last stopping-place.This accounted satisfactorily for Sailor Ben's singu-lar movements, and considerably calmed my fears.Nevertheless, I did not like the aspect of things.

The Admiral continued to snooze like a goodfellow, and was snoring melodiously as we glidedat a slackened pace over a bridge and into Boston.I grasped my pilgrim's bundle, and, hurryingout of the car, dashed up the first street that pre-sented itself.

IV

The Admiral on Guard

It was a narrow, noisy, zigzag street, crowdedwith trucks and obstructed with bales and boxesof merchandise. I did not pause to breathe untilI had placed a respectable distance between meand the railway station. By this time it wasnearly twilight.

I had got into the region of dwelling-houses,and was about to seat myself on a doorstep torest, when, lo! there was the Admiral trundlingalong on the opposite sidewalk, under a full spreadof canvas, as he would have expressed it.

I was off again in an instant at a rapid pace;but in spite of all I could do he held his own with-out any perceptible exertion. He had a very uglygait to get away from, the Admiral. I did not dareto run, for fear of being mistaken for a thief, asuspicion which my bundle would naturally lendcolor to.

I pushed ahead, however, at a brisk trot, andmust have got over one or two miles — my pur-suer neither gaining nor losing ground — when Iconcluded to surrender at discretion. I saw thatSailor Ben was determined to have me, and, know-ing my man, I knew that escape was highly im-probable.

So I turned round and waited for him to catchup with me, which he did in a few seconds, look-ing rather sheepish at first.

" Sailor Ben," said I severely, " do I understandthat you are dogging my steps ?"

" Well, little messmate," replied the Admiral,rubbing his nose, which he always did when hewas disconcerted, "I am kind o' followin' in yourwake."

" Under orders ?"

" Under orders."

" Under the Captain's orders ? "

" Surely."

" In other words, my grandfather has sent youto fetch me back to Rivermouth ?'

"That's about it," said the Admiral, with aburst of frankness.

" And I must go with you whether I want to ornot ?"

" The Capen's very identical words !'

There was nothing to be done. I bit my lipswith suppressed anger, and signified that I was athis disposal, since I could not help it. The im-pression was very strong in my mind that theAdmiral would not hesitate to put me in irons ifI showed signs of mutiny.

It was too late to return to Rivermouth thatnight — a fact which I communicated to the oldboy sullenly, inquiring at the same time what heproposed to do about it.

He said we would cruise about for some rations,and then make a night of it. I did not condescendto reply, though I hailed the suggestion of some-thing to eat with inward enthusiasm, for I had nottaken enough food that day to keep life in a canary.

We wandered back to the railway station, inthe waiting-room of which was a kind of restaurantpresided over by a severe - looking young lady.Here we had a cup of coffee apiece, several toughdoughnuts, and some blocks of venerable sponge-cake. The young lady who attended on us, what-ever her age was then, must have been a merechild when that sponge-cake was made.

The Admiral's acquaintance with Boston hotelswas slight; but he knew of a quiet lodging-housenear by, much patronized by sea-captains, andkept by a former friend of his.

In this house, which had seen its best days, wewere accommodated with a mouldy chamber con-taining two cot-beds, two chairs, and a crackedpitcher on a washstand. The mantel-shelf wasornamented with three big pink conch-shells, re-sembling pieces of petrified liver; and over thesehung a cheap lurid print, in which a United Statessloop-of-war was giving a British frigate particularfits. It is very strange how our own ships neverseem to suffer any in these terrible engagements.It shows what a nation we are.

An oil-lamp on a deal-table cast a dismal glareover the apartment, which was cheerless in theextreme. I thought of our sitting-room at home,with its flowery wall-paper and gay curtains andsoft lounges; I saw Major Elkanah Nutter (mygrandfather's father) in powdered wig and Fed-eral uniform, looking down benevolently from his

gilt frame between the bookcases; I picturedthe Captain and Miss Abigail sitting at the cosyround table in the moonlight glow of the astrallamp ; and then I fell to wondering how theywould receive me when I came back. I wonderedif the Prodigal Son had any idea that his fatherwas going to kill the fatted calf for him, and howhe felt about it, on the whole.

Though I was very low in spirits, I put on abold front to Sailor Ben, you will understand. Tobe caught and caged in this manner was a fright-ful shock to my vanity. He tried to draw me intoconversation ; but I answered in icy monosyllables.He again suggested we should make a night ofit, and hinted broadly that he was game for anyamount of riotous dissipation, even to the extentof going to see a play if I wanted to. I declinedhaughtily. I was dying to go.

He then threw out a feeler on the subject ofdominoes and checkers, and observed in a generalway that " seven up " was a capital game; but Irepulsed him at every point.

I saw that the Admiral was beginning to feelhurt by my systematic coldness. We had alwaysbeen such hearty friends until now. It was toobad of me to fret that tender, honest old hearteven for an hour. I really did love the ancientboy, and when in a disconsolate way he orderedup a pitcher of beer, I unbent so far as to partakeof some in a teacup. He recovered his spirits

instantly, and took out his cuddy clay pipe for asmoke.

Between the beer and the soothing fragranceof the navy-plug, I fell into a pleasanter moodmyself, and, it being too late now to go to the

 Playing "Seven Up"

theatre, I condescended to say — addressing the northwest corner of the ceiling — that " seven up "was a capital game. Upon this hint the Admiral disappeared, and returned shortly with a very dirty pack of cards.

As we played, with varying fortunes, by the flickering flame of the lamp, he sipped his beer and became communicative. He seemed im-mensely tickled by the fact that I had come to Boston. It leaked out presently that he and the Captain had had a wager on the subject.

The discovery of my plans and who had dis-covered them were points on which the Admiral refused to throw any light. They had been dis-covered, however, and the Captain had laughed at the idea of my running away. Sailor Ben, on the contrary, had stoutly contended that I meant to slip cable and be off. Whereupon the captain offered to bet him a dollar that I would not go. And it was partly on account of this wager that Sailor Ben refrained from capturing me when he might have done so at the start.

Now, as the fare to and from Boston, with the lodging expenses, would cost at least five dollars, I did not see what he gained by winning the wager. The Admiral rubbed his nose violently when this view of the case presented itself.

I asked him why he did not take me from the train at the first stopping-place and return to Rivermouth by the down train at 4.30. He ex-plained : having purchased a ticket for Boston, he considered himself bound to the owners (the stock-holders of the road) to fulfill his part of the con-tract. To use his own words, he had "shipped for the viage."

This struck me as being so deliciously funny, that after I was in bed and the light was out I could not help laughing aloud once or twice. I suppose the Admiral must have thought I was meditating another escape, for he made periodical visits to my bed throughout the night, satisfying himself by kneading me all over that I had not evaporated.

I was all there the next morning, when Sailor Ben half awakened me by shouting merrily, " All hands on deck !' The words rang in my ears like a part of my own dream, for I was at that in-stant climbing up the side of the Rawlings to offer myself as cabin-boy.

The Admiral was obliged to shake me roughlytwo or three times before he could detach mefrom the dream. I opened my eyes with effort,and stared stupidly round the room. Bit by bitmy real situation dawned on me. What a sick-ening sensation that is, when one is in trouble, towake up feeling free for a moment, and then tofind yesterday's sorrow all ready to go on again!

" Well, little messmate, how fares it ?"

I was too much depressed to reply. Thethought of returning to Rivermouth chilled me.How could I face Captain Nutter, to say nothingof Miss Abigail and Kitty ? How the TempleGrammar School boys would look at me ! HowConway and Seth Rodgers would exult over mymortification! And what if the Rev. WibirdHawkins should allude to me in his next Sun-day's sermon ?

Sailor Ben was wise in keeping an eye on me,for after these thoughts took possession of mymind, I wanted only the opportunity to give himthe slip.

The keeper of the lodgings did not supplymeals to his guests ; so we breakfasted at a smallchop-house in a crooked street on our way to thecars. The city was not astir yet, and lookedglum and careworn in the damp morning atmos-phere.

Here and there as we passed along was a sharp-faced shop-boy taking down shutters; and nowand then we met a seedy man who had evidentlyspent the night in a doorway. Such early birdsand a few laborers with their tin kettles were theonly signs of life to be seen until we came to thestation, where I insisted on paying for my ownticket. I did not relish being conveyed fromplace to place, like a felon changing prisons, atsomebody else's expense.

On entering the car I sunk into a seat next thewindow, and Sailor Ben deposited himself besideme, cutting off all chance of escape.

The car filled up soon after this, and I won-dered if there was anything in my mien that wouldlead the other passengers to suspect I was a boywho had run away and was being brought back.

A man in front of us — he was near-sighted, asI discovered later by his reading a guide-book withhis nose — brought the blood to my cheeks by turning round and peering at me steadily. Irubbed a clear spot on the cloudy window-glassat my elbow, and looked out to avoid him.

There, in the travelers' room, was the severe-looking young lady pil-ing up her blocks ofsponge-cake in allur-ing pyramids and in-dustriously intrench-ing herself behind abreastwork of squash-pie. I saw with pleas-ure numerous victimswalk up to the coun-ter and recklessly sowthe seeds of deathin their constitutionsby eating her dough-nuts. I had got quite interested in her, when the whistle sounded andthe train began to move.

The Admiral and I did not talk much on thejourney. I stared out of the window most of thetime, speculating as to the probable nature ofthe reception in store for me at the terminus ofthe road.

What would the Captain say ? and Mr. Grim-shaw, what would he do about it ? Then I thoughtof Pepper Whitcomb. Dire was the vengeance Imeant to wreak on Pepper, for who but he had

The Near-Sighted Man

betrayed me ? Pepper alone had been the reposi-tory of my secret —perfidious Pepper!

As we left station after station behind us, I feltless and less like encountering the members ofour family. Sailor Ben fathomed what was pass-ing in my mind, for he leaned over and said :

" I don't think as the Capen will bear down veryhard on you."

But it was not that. It was not the fear of anyphysical punishment that might be inflicted ; itwas the sense of my own folly that was creepingover me; for during the long, silent ride I hadexamined my conduct from every standpoint, andthere was no view I could take of myself in whichI did not look like a very foolish person indeed.

As we came within sight of the spires of River-mouth, I would not have cared if the up train,which met us outside the town, had run into usand ended me.

Contrary to my expectation and dread, the Cap-tain was not visible when we stepped from thecars. Sailor Ben glanced among the crowd offaces, apparently looking for him too. Conwaywas there — he was always hanging about the sta-tion — and if he had intimated in any way that heknew of my disgrace and enjoyed it, I shouldhave walked into him, I am certain.

But this defiant feeling entirely deserted me bythe time we reached the Nutter House. TheCaptain himself opened the door.

" Come on board, sir," said Sailor Ben, scrapinghis left foot and touching his hat sea-fashion.

My grandfather nodded to Sailor Ben, some-what coldly I thought, and much to my astonish-ment kindly took me by the hand.

I was unprepared for this, and the tears, whichno amount of severity would have wrung from me,welled up to my eyes.

The expression of my grandfather's face, as Iglanced at it hastily, was grave and gentle; therewas nothing in it of anger or reproof. I followedhim into the sitting-room, and, obeying a motionof his hand, seated myself on the sofa. He re-mained standing by the round table for a moment,lost in thought, then leaned over and picked up aletter.

It was a letter with a great black seal.

CHAPTER XXI

IN WHICH I LEAVE RIVERMOUTH

A LETTER with a great black seal!

I knew then what had happened as well as Iknow it now. But which was it, father or mother ?I do not like to look back to the agony and sus-pense of that moment.

My father had died at New Orleans during one of his weekly visits to the city. The letter bear-ing these tidings had reached Rivermouth the evening of my flight — had passed me on the road by the down train.

I must turn back for a moment to that eventful evening. When I failed to make my appearance at supper, the Captain began to suspect that I had really started on my wild tour southward — a conjecture which Sailor Ben's absence helped to confirm. I had evidently got off by the train and Sailor Ben had followed me.

There was no telegraphic communication be-tween Boston and Rivermouth in those days; so my grandfather could do nothing but await the result. Even if there had been another mail to Boston, he could not have availed himself of it, not knowing how to address a message to the

fugitives. The post-office was naturally the last place either I or the Admiral would think of vis-iting.

My grandfather, however, was too full of trouble to allow this to add to his distress. He knew that the faithful old sailor would not let me come to any harm, and even if I had managed for the time being to elude him, was sure to bring me back sooner or later.

Our return, therefore, by the first train on the following day did not surprise him.

I was greatly puzzled, as I have said, by the gentle manner of his reception ; but when we were alone together in the sitting-room, and he began slowly to unfold the letter, I understood it all. I caught a sight of my mother's handwriting in the superscription, and there was nothing left to tell me.

My grandfather held the letter a few seconds irresolutely, and then commenced reading it aloud; but he could get no further than the date.

" I can't read it, Tom," said the old gentleman, breaking down. " I thought I could."

He handed it to me. I took the letter mechan-ically, and hurried away with it to my little room, where I had passed so many happy hours.

The week that followed the receipt of this letter is nearly a blank in my memory. I remember that the days appeared endless; that at times I could not realize the misfortune that had befallen us,

and my heart upbraided me for not feeling a deeper grief; that a full sense of my loss would now and then sweep over me like an inspiration, and I would steal away to my chamber or wander for-lornly about the gardens. I remember this, but little more.

As the days went by my first grief subsided, and in its place grew up a want which I have ex-perienced at every step in life from boyhood to manhood. Often, even now, after all these years,

My First Grief

when I see a lad of twelve or fourteen walking by his father's side, and glancing merrily up at his face, I turn and look after them, and am conscious that I have missed companionship most sweet and sacred.

I shall not dwell on this portion of my story, There were many tranquil, pleasant hours in store for me at that period, and I prefer to turn to them.

One evening the Captain came smiling into the sitting-room with an open letter in his hand. My mother had arrived at New York, and would be with us the next day. For the first time in weeks— years, it seemed to me —something of the old cheerfulness mingled with our conversation round the evening lamp. I was to go to Boston with the Captain to meet her and bring her home. I need not describe that meeting. With my mother's hand in mine once more, all the long years we had been parted appeared like a dream. Very dear to me was the sight of that slender, pale woman passing from room to room, and lending a patient grace and beauty to the saddened life of the old house.

Everything was changed with us now. There were consultations with lawyers, and signing of papers, and correspondence ; for my father's affairs had been left in great confusion. And when these were settled, the evenings were not long enough for us to hear all my mother had to tell of the scenes she had passed through in the ill-fated city.

Then there were old times to talk over, full of reminiscences of Aunt Chloe and little Black Sam. Little Black Sam, by the by, had been taken by

his master from my father's service ten months previously, and put on a sugar-plantation near Baton Rouge. Not relishing the change, Sam had run away, and by some mysterious agency got into ,Canada, from which place he had sent back several indecorous messages to his late owner. Aunt Chloe was still in New Orleans, employed as nurse in one of the cholera hospital wards, and the Des-moulins, near neighbors of ours, had purchased the pretty brick house among the orange-trees.

How all these simple details interested me will be readily understood by any boy who has been long absent from home.

I was sorry when it became necessary to discuss questions more nearly affecting myself. I had been removed from school temporarily, but it was de-cided, after much consideration, that I should not return, the decision being left, in a manner, in my own hands.

The Captain wished to carry out his son's inten-tion and send me to college, as I was fully prepared to undergo the preliminary examinations. This, however, would have been a heavy drain on the modest income reverting to my mother after the settlement of my father's estate, and the

Captainproposed to take the expense upon himself, notseeing clearly what other disposal to make of me.

In the midst of our discussions a letter camefrom my Uncle Snow, a merchant in New York,generously offering me a place in his counting-

house. The case resolved itself into this: If Iwent to college, I should have to devote severalyears to my studies, and at the end of the collegi-ate course would have no settled profession. If Iaccepted my uncle's offer, which could not standwaiting, I should at once be in a comparativelyindependent position. It was hard to give up thelong-cherished dream of being a Harvard boy ; butI gave it up.

The decision once made, it was Uncle Snow'swish that I should enter his counting-house im-mediately. The cause of my good uncle's hastewas this: he was afraid that I would turn out tobe a poet before he could make a merchant of me.

His fears were based upon the fact that I hadpublished in the Rivermouth Barnacle some versesaddressed in a familiar manner " To the Moon."Now, the idea of a boy, with his living to get,placing himself in communication with the Moon,struck the mercantile mind as monstrous. It wasnot only a bad investment, it was lunacy.

We adopted Uncle Snow's views so far as toaccede to his proposition forthwith. My mother,I neglected to say, was also to reside in NewYork.

I shall not draw a picture of Pepper Whitcomb'sdisgust when the news was imparted to him, norattempt to paint Sailor Ben's distress at the pros-pect of losing his little messmate.

In the excitement of preparing for the journey

I did not feel any very deep regret myself. Butwhen the moment came for leaving, and I saw mysmall trunk lashed up behind the carriage, thenthe pleasantness of the old life and a vague dreadof the new came over me, and a mist filled myeyes, shutting out the group of schoolfellows, in-cluding all the members of the Centipede Club,who had come down to the house to see me off.

As the carriage swept round the corner, I leanedout of the window to take a last look at SailorBen's cottage, and there was the Admiral's flagflying at half-mast.

So I left Rivermouth, little dreaming that I wasnot to see the old place again for many and manya year.

CHAPTER XXII

EXEUNT OMNES

WITH the close of my schooldays at Rivermouththis modest chronicle ends.

The new life upon which I entered, the newfriends and foes I encountered on the road, andwhat I did and what I did not, are matters thatdo not come within the scope of these pages. Butbefore I write Finis to the record as it stands,before I leave it — feeling as if I were once moregoing away from my boyhood — I have a word ortwo to say concerning a few of the personageswho have figured in the story, if you will allow meto call Gypsy a personage.

I am sure that the reader who has followed methus far will be willing to hear what became of her,and Sailor Ben and Miss Abigail and the Captain.

First about Gypsy. A month after my depar-ture from Rivermouth the Captain informed meby letter that he had parted with the little mare,according to agreement. She had been sold tothe ring-master of a traveling circus (I had stipu-lated on this disposal of her), anJ was about to setout on her travels. She did not disappoint myglowing anticipations, but became quite a celebrity in her way, by dancing the polka to slow music on a pine-board ball-room constructed for the purpose. I chanced once, a long while afterwards, to be in a country town where her troupe was giving exhibitions; I even read the gaudily illumined show-bill, setting forth the accomplishments of

FORMfRLY OWNCOTHE. PfUNC£eSHA7-Z.AN|AN

— but failed to recognize my dear little mustang girl behind those high-sounding titles, and so, alas! did not attend the performance. I hope all the

praises she received and all the spangled trappings she wore did not spoil her; but I am afraid they did, for she was always over much given to the vanities of this world.

Miss Abigail regulated the domestic destinies of my grandfather's household until the day of her death, which Dr. Theophilus Tredick solemnly averred was hastened by the inveterate habit she had contracted of swallowing unknown quantities of hot-drops whenever she fancied herself out of sorts. Eighty-seven empty phials were found in a bonnet-box on a shelf in her bedroom closet.

The old house became very lonely when the family got reduced to Captain Nutter and Kitty; and when Kitty passed away, my grandfather di-vided his time between Rivermouth and New York.

Sailor Ben did not long survive his little Irish lass, as he always fondly called her. At his de-mise, which took place about six years ago, he left his property in trust to the managers of a "Home for Aged Mariners." In his will, which was a very whimsical document — written by him-self, and worded with much shrewdness, too — he warned the Trustees that when he got "aloft" he intended to keep his "weather eye" on them, and should send "a speritual shot across their bows" and bring them to, if they did n't treat the Aged Mariners handsomely.

He also expressed a wish to have his body

stitched up in a shotted hammock and dropped into the harbor; but as he did not strenuously insiston this, and as it was not in accordance with mygrandfather's preconceived notions of Christianburial, the Admiral was laid to rest beside Kitty,in the Old South Burying Ground, with an an-chor that would have delighted him neatly carvedon his headstone.

I am sorry the fire has gone out in the old ship'sstove in that sky-blue cottage at the head of thewharf; I am sorry they have taken down the flag-staff and painted over the port-holes; for I lovedthe old cabin as it was. They might have let italone !

For several months after leaving RivermouthI carried on a voluminous correspondence withPepper Whitcomb ; but it gradually dwindled downto a single letter a month, and then to none at all.But while he remained at the Temple GrammarSchool he kept me advised of the current gossipof the town and the doings of the Centipedes.

As one by one the boys left the academy —Adams, Harris, Harden, Blake, and Langdon —to seek their fortunes elsewhere, there was less tointerest me in the old seaport; and when Pepperhimself went to Philadelphia to read law, I had noone to give me an inkling of what was going on.

There was not much to go on, to be sure.Great events no longer considered it worth theirwhile to honor so quiet a place. One Fourth of

July the Temple Grammar School burnt down —-set on fire, it was supposed, by an eccentric squibthat was seen to dart into an upper window— andMr. Grimshaw retired from public life, married," and lived happily ever after," as the story-bookssay.

The Widow Conway, I am able to state, did notsucceed in enslaving Mr. Meeks, the apothecary,who united himself clandestinely to one of MissDorothy Gibbs's young ladies, and lost the patron-age of Primrose Hall in consequence.

Young Conway went into the grocery businesswith his ancient chum, Rodgers — RODGERS &CONWAY ! I read the sign only last summer whenI was down in Rivermouth, and had half a mind topop into the shop and shake hands with him, andask him if he wanted to fight. I contented my-self, however, with flattening my nose against hisdingy shop-window, and beheld Conway, in redwhiskers and blue overalls, weighing out sugar fora customer — giving him short weight, I wouldbet anything !

I have reserved my pleasantest word for the last.It is touching the Captain. The Captain is stillhale and rosy, and if he does not relate his exploitin the war of 1812 as spiritedly as he used to, hemakes up by relating it more frequently and tell-ing it differently every time. He passes his win-ters in New York and his summers in the NutterHouse, which threatens to prove a hard nut for

the destructive gentleman with the scythe and thehour-glass, for the seaward gable has not yieldeda clapboard to the east wind these twenty years.The Captain has now become the Oldest Inhab-itant in Rivermouth, and so I do not laugh at theOldest Inhabitant any more, but pray in my heartthat he may occupy the post of honor for half acentury to come !

So ends the Story of a Bad Boy — but not sucha very bad boy, as I told you to begin with.

THE END

Manufactured by Amazon.ca
Bolton, ON

19811135R00068